Christmas
at
Hilltop Inn

PAT NICHOLS

Christmas at Hilltop Inn by Pat Nichols
Published by Armchair Press
ISBN: 979-8-9912411-1-3
Copyright © 2024 by Pat Nichols
Cover Design by Elaina Lee
Edited by Sherri Stewart

Available in print from your local bookstore or online.
For more information on this book or the author visit:
https://patnicholsauthor.blog
Printed in the United States of America
is a work of fiction. Names, characters, and incidents are all
products of the author's imagination or are used for fictional
Christmas at Hilltop Inn purposes. Any mentioned brand
names, places, and trademarks remain the property of their
respective owners, bear no association with the author or
publisher, and are used for fictional purposes only.
Library of Congress Cataloging-in Publication Data
Nichols, Pat.
Christmas at Hilltop Inn / Pat Nichols

Books by
Pat Nichols

Women's Fiction

Blue Ridge Series

Blizzard at Blue Ridge Inn
The Inheritance
The Wedding
Christmas at Hilltop Inn
More titles in 2025

Butler Family Legacy Series

Big Secrets, Little Lies
Truth and Forgiveness
New Beginnings

Willow Falls Series

The Secret of Willow Inn
Trouble in Willow Falls
Starstruck in Willow Falls
Bridges, Books, and Bones

Dedicated to my beautiful mother Bette Hamilton whose favorite holiday was Christmas. One day we will celebrate together again in eternity.

Chapter 1

A western wind triggered by dark clouds nipped Erica Nelson's cheeks as she stepped onto the eighteenth green at the Toccoa Hills golf course. She pointed to a ball. "Is the one closest to the hole mine?"

"Your best shot yet." Brad Barkley's blue eyes lit with a smile.

"If I sink it, I'll accomplish my first ever one-stroke putt." Two months ago, she had swung a golf club for the first time in her life. Now she understood all the hullabaloo about the game.

Her golf partner removed the flag whipping in the wind. "Slow and steady."

"Thanks, Coach." She eyed the target three feet away. Reading the green the way Brad had taught her, she tapped the ball. Erica held her breath as the ball curved across the turf and fell into the hole. She released the air. "Wow, my first one-stroke putt."

"Congratulations." He retrieved her ball. "You finished today's game one stroke better than last week."

Erica brushed her dark hair away from her cheek. "Maybe one day I'll break a hundred."

"You've come a long way during the last six weeks."

"Thanks to your patience and expert coaching."

"Mastering this game is a lifelong quest, and today is only the third time you've played eighteen holes." Brad handed Erica the flag, then sank a long putt.

"Impressive."

"Thanks." Brad retrieved his ball.

"At least we finished before the storm." After Erica replaced the flag, they scurried from the green to their golf cart. She dropped her rented putter into the bag. "Did you teach your wife to play?"

"Actually, Jan taught me and our two boys. You can bet if there's a golf course in heaven, she's playing every day with her dad."

"Neither of the men I married were golfers." Erica climbed into the cart. "Gunter was too busy gambling and juggling three separate lives."

Brad slid in beside her. "I still don't understand how he managed three aliases to keep three intelligent women in the dark all those years."

"Gunter was a master at deception. Amanda and I each married him to provide for our daughters. Wendy was swept off her feet by his charm and promise of a luxurious lifestyle."

"At least now he's behind bars on the other side of the country."

"For killing a loan shark—not for bigamy and stealing everything from his three wives."

"Whatever the reason, Gunter Benson is where he belongs." Brad steered the cart toward the pro shop. "Was your first husband a sports fan?"

"Jack was obsessed with boxing." Erica removed her golf glove. "Unfortunately, I became his punching bag."

"Any man who hits a woman or a child belongs behind bars."

"Unless he's a cop protected by his pals. Enough talk about my poor choices in men."

Brad chuckled. "Does your description include a certain high school principal?"

Erica's gaze slid to Brad's curly dark brown hair. "Would you believe you're my first male pal?"

"I'll accept your comment as a compliment." They returned to the golf cart and stowed Brad's clubs in his SUV, then made their way to the outdoor bar. He ordered a beer. Erica opted for a glass of chardonnay. "How's your daughter's volunteer work going at the crisis center?"

"Abby loves tutoring those kids."

"Seems she's found her calling."

Erica averted her eyes. "I'll never forget Abby's expression eleven years ago when I asked what she'd wished for when she blew out the candles on her birthday cake. My innocent seven-year-old child looked at me with the saddest eyes I had ever seen and said, 'I prayed for Daddy not to kill you, Mommy.' Later, after Jack left to go on duty, we packed two suitcases and fled to a women's shelter. Four months later, Jack agreed to an uncontested divorce to protect his career." Erica swallowed a sip of wine to quench her dry throat. "The kind woman who tutored Abby during our stay at the shelter had a profound impact on her career choice."

"Other than my wife, you and your daughter are two of the strongest women I have ever known."

"I'm sorry I didn't have the chance to know her."

"You and she would have become good friends. Jimmy takes after his mother. He's sensitive and tenderhearted. Which is why he's struggling after losing both his job and his girlfriend in the same week."

"Is he planning to move back to Blue Ridge, or just stay with you a little while longer?"

Brad wrapped his fingers around his beer. "Right now, he's dealing with too much depression to make a long-term decision."

"He's fortunate to have you as a father."

3

"Jimmy's a good kid with a lot of potential. I'm treating him to dinner at Grace Prime Steakhouse tonight." Brad sipped his beer. "Enough about that. One of these days you'll need to buy a set of golf clubs."

Erica grinned. "So you assume I'll continue playing?"

"Here's hoping you will. Especially since you've given me the perfect excuse to add Sunday afternoon back to my weekly golf schedule."

"Well then, I can't let my coach down. Although, I'll need a lot more months of salary from Hilltop Inn before I can afford a set of clubs."

"Top quality clubs don't come cheap." Brad fell silent for a long moment. His eyes dulled. "My wife's clubs have been sitting in a closet collecting dust for three years." He faced Erica. "Jan would want my friend to have them."

The sadness in Brad's eyes tugged on Erica's heart. If she accepted the gift, would the pain of losing his wife to cancer resurface every time they played?

"Being able to talk to you about Jan has helped me recover from the pain of losing her." Brad touched Erica's arm. "I want you to have her clubs."

Her shoulders tensed. "Are you sure?"

"A month ago, I wasn't strong enough to say yes. Now, I am."

Was he? She wouldn't turn down something that meant so much to him. "I accept your generous gift with gratitude."

A smile played on his lips. "Next Sunday, you'll play with top-notch equipment."

"And maybe shave another stroke off my game."

"Now you're talking as if you've played golf for years."

"I'm a fast learner."

"Next week, we'll celebrate your progress with dinner." He withdrew his hand and swallowed the last of his beer. "Now, I need to head home."

Erica took one more sip of wine, then slid off her stool.

The rain began during their ride back to town. By the time they pulled into the ranch house carport, a full-blown storm released a deluge. He dashed to the passenger side and opened the door. "Perfect timing."

Erica climbed out. "Thank you for another enjoyable Sunday afternoon."

"Likewise. Same time next week?"

"Absolutely." Erica waved over her shoulder as she strode through the carport to the kitchen door. Abby's golden retriever greeted her with an enthusiastic tail wag. She patted Dusty's head, then headed to the living room she had transformed into a proper office. Dusty padded behind her and sprawled on the floor. Erica eyed her business card lying on the desk. Erica Nelson, CEO Awesam. The way Wendy combined the names Amanda, Wendy, Erica, Abby, and Morgan to create their company name still made her smile. She opened her laptop and pulled up her schedule. One guest had booked a massage for tomorrow afternoon.

Footsteps struck the den floor, and Amanda Smith breezed in. "There's a real gulley washer going on." She plopped onto a chair beside the desk. "How's your golf game coming along?"

Erica swiveled toward her partner. "Brad plans to give me his wife's golf clubs."

"Hmm." Amanda ran her fingers through her red hair.

"Don't read anything into his gesture."

"I'm not."

"Yes, you are."

Amanda shrugged. "If I am—which is a big if—who can blame me?"

"Brad and I are friends, nothing more."

"For now."

Erica rolled her eyes. "You're hopeless."

A lightning flash followed by a thunderclap sent Dusty scrambling onto Erica's lap. She gently pushed the sixty-five-pound dog onto the floor. "I don't know about you two, but I'm hungry."

Dusty whimpered as she followed them to the kitchen.

Amanda removed leftover lasagna from the fridge. "Are you comfortable accepting Jan's clubs from Brad?"

Erica shrugged. "He's giving me a generous gift."

"You didn't answer my question."

"Because I don't know. How about we change the subject."

"To what?" Amanda tossed Dusty a dog biscuit.

"Anything other than golf or Brad, and don't read something into my request."

"Fair enough." Amanda plated two slices of lasagna and set them in the microwave. "We have a full house next door."

"Millie will need both of us to help serve breakfast to our fourteen guests." A thunderclap shook the house a second after a lightning flash. "Talk about too close." Erica stroked Dusty's back. The microwave dinged. "At least we didn't lose power."

Fifteen minutes after they settled at the dining room table in the den, distant sirens grew louder until the shrill wail drowned out Dusty's whimper and sent a shiver up Erica's spine.

Chapter 2

Amanda bolted from her chair, raced to the kitchen, and yanked the back door open. Two fire engines drove past their house then slowed. The acrid odor of smoke wafted across the carport.

"Is the inn on fire?" Erica's tone hinted of fear.

"The engines drove past the inn." Amanda grabbed her umbrella and raced between Abby's car and the truck she and Erica shared. A third fire truck passed the ranch house and braked behind the other two.

Erica opened her umbrella and raced across the inn's front lawn behind Amanda. Hilltop Inn guests gathered on the front porch gawking at the flames and thick black smoke shooting from the back of Millie Cunningham's house. Firefighters scrambled to connect a hose and drag it across the front yard and around the side of the house.

Their neighbor stood frozen at the edge of her property cradling her two cats in her arms. Wet strands of salt and pepper hair were plastered to her cheek. Water dripped off the tip of her nose. Her soaked shirt clung to her thin body.

Amanda held her umbrella over the woman who served as Hilltop's breakfast chef. "What happened?"

"Lightning struck my house and scared me and my cats half to death."

Amanda blinked at the smoke stinging her eyes. "Are you okay?"

Millie shivered. "The home I've lived in for more than fifty years is on fire. What do you think?"

Amanda slid her arm around Millie's trembling shoulders. "I meant are you hurt?"

"I stubbed my pinkie toe, which hurts like the dickens. Otherwise, I'm okay. At least physically."

A firefighter released a nozzle, sending a high-powered stream of water into the flames. Two more firefighters hauled a hose around the garage and added a second torrent of water.

The women remained silent amid the flurry of activity. A river of ashes snaked down the yard into the street. The glow from the fire-engine lights reflected in the wet road as the acrid odor of charred wood hung heavy in the night air. At some point the downpour ebbed to a gentle rain. The black smoke pouring through the roof gave way to a billow of white steam.

Moments after the visible flames disappeared, Millie headed to her back-yard. Amanda and Erica followed. After the professionals doused hot spots with foam, a soot-covered firefighter approached. "The fire was mostly contained in the kitchen and one bedroom, Mrs. Cunningham. Unfortunately, the smoke and water damage did a number on the other rooms and will require a lot of repairs."

With a tremulous sigh, Millie surveyed her damaged home. "When can I go inside?"

"Tomorrow, but only if we determine the structure safe. Do you have someplace to go until your home is repaired?"

Erica nodded. "She'll stay at our house."

Millie's brows pinched. "I don't want to be a burden."

"You won't be." Erica cast her eyes on Amanda. "Right, partner?"

Amanda hesitated. A burden? Maybe not. A constant thorn in her side? Definitely. A coughing fit assailed her.

Millie cut her a sideways glare. "I'll stay with my son—"

"Nonsense." Amanda shook water off her umbrella. "He lives a half hour away in the middle of nowhere. Besides, you don't need to drive on those curvy roads before dawn when you can walk across a driveway to work."

"Amanda's right." Erica nudged Millie's arm. "Since Wendy's married, we have a spare bedroom."

"You also have a dog, and I have two cats."

Amanda shrugged. "Seems we'll manage a domestic-animal zoo for a while."

"Until Dusty attacks one of my kitties."

"Yeah, well, one of your kitties is far more likely to harass Dusty."

Erica nudged Millie. "Seems my role as Awesam's peacemaker is back in demand."

Millie's brow pinched. "What are you really saying?"

"Before Wendy moved out, she and Amanda butted heads all the time. For however long it takes to repair your home, you'll assume our CFO's role as our president's number-one test of much-needed patience."

Amanda stifled a laugh. "And Erica's skill as a mediator."

"Hmph. If I stay with you, I'll need a new kitty-litter box."

"Tonight?"

Millie rolled her eyes. "You obviously don't know beans about cats."

"Seems I'm about to learn. Tell you what—after we take you home, I'll head over to Walmart and buy whatever you need for tonight."

"I'll make you a list."

"In the meantime, we need to dry off while our first responders finish their job." The women spun around and headed back across the inn's front lawn.

"Is that your house, Millie?" A guest called out from the front porch.

"I'm afraid so. Don't worry, I'll serve a delicious breakfast tomorrow morning."

Amanda nudged their chef's arm. "If you want to take tomorrow off, Erica and I will fix breakfast for our guests."

"Other than your spaghetti sauce, neither of you have a clue how to fix fancy food worthy of a five-star inn. Besides, I need to stay busy to keep my mind off my damaged home."

"While you're staying with us, you should teach me and Erica how to cook."

"The same way I taught Wendy?"

"Exactly."

"What would you two do without me?"

"I suppose we'd serve guests mediocre breakfasts and ruin our inn's reputation." Amanda opened the kitchen door. Dusty raced in from the den, barking. Millie's calico hissed. "We need to keep your cats behind closed doors, at least for tonight." She led their chef to Wendy's room. "What are their names?"

"My calico is Whiskers. The other one is Mittens—because of her white front paws." Millie released her pets. Whiskers leapt onto the windowsill while Mittens shimmied under the bed. "About my list."

Twenty minutes later, Amanda climbed into the truck and called Wendy. "You won't believe what's going on." She relayed everything that had happened during the past two hours.

"Oh my gosh. How bad is the damage?"

"We'll know more tomorrow."

"How are you gonna handle living under the same roof with Millie?"

"I'll rely on Erica to keep the peace." Amanda backed down the driveway. "How's my grandson?"

"Missing his nana. I'll bring him over tomorrow morning."

Amanda smiled. Unofficially adopting Wendy as her second daughter had been a blessing to both of them. "I can't wait to hold him."

"Thanks for bringing me into the loop about the fire. Let me know what I can do to help."

"Will do." Amanda ended the call as she braked at the stop sign and turned toward town. One fact was certain. Millie and her cats would test her patience to the limit.

After finding every item on Millie's list, Amanda drove back to the ranch house. She parked beside Abby's car and hauled the purchases into the kitchen. Millie—wearing Erica's bathrobe—sat at the dining room table in the den. Amanda set the purchases on the floor beside her chair. "I found everything on your list."

"I'll pay you back tomorrow."

"No hurry." Amanda settled beside Hilltop's chef. "Wendy's bringing baby Ryan over tomorrow morning."

Millie's eyes glazed over as she heaved a dolorous sigh. "Rupert and I built our house before our son was born. His crib is still in the attic...oh no." Millie pressed her hand to her throat. "Eleanor Harrington's journals—" Her tone screamed with alarm. "That last summer she and her husband stayed in their vacation house she left them behind so I'd find them. I'll never forgive myself if they're ruined."

Amanda's mind drifted to the day Wendy discovered the journals in the downstairs bedroom they had transformed into the Rainbow Suite. "Where are they?"

"In my bedroom, at the front of the house."

"Given the fire was contained in the kitchen and back bedroom, they're probably untouched."

"I couldn't bear to lose those." Millie's hand dropped to her lap. "The lightning bolt missed the inn and struck my house as atonement for my secret affair with a married man all those years ago."

"Nonsense." Amanda touched Millie's arm. "Lightning is a random act of nature, not some sort of punishment."

"When I married Rupert, I still believed my lover would leave his wife and take me away. By the time I accepted the truth, I had damaged my marriage beyond repair." Their chef grabbed a glass of water and took a long drink. "Rupert turned into an old curmudgeon because of me."

"You and your husband stayed together—"

"For our son, not for me."

Amanda patted their partner's arm. "You wouldn't have stayed together if you didn't love each other at least a little."

Millie's eyes narrowed. "If you're trying to make me feel better, forget it. I know I'm not the easiest person to get along with."

"You know what?" Amanda withdrew her hand. "You're right, but we all love you anyway."

Millie stared wide-eyed at Amanda then released a nervous chuckle. "You're right about the two of us testing Erica's peacemaker skills. Starting tomorrow. Tonight, I'm going to set up my kitties' litter box then go to bed."

"Do you need my help?"

"I've lived alone for years." Millie scooped the bags off the table and headed toward Wendy's room. "Believe me, I'm capable of managing on my own."

"All right then, I'll see you in the morning."

Erica walked in, dropped onto the sofa, and leaned back.. "She's been here for an hour and I'm already exhausted."

Amanda heaved a sigh. "At least the three of us aren't allergic to cats. Millie's another story."

Chapter 3

S atisfied with her progress, Wendy Armstrong logged off her online course and closed her laptop. She tiptoed from her and Chris's home office into the nursery across the hall. Baby Ryan slept peacefully in his crib beneath the jungle safari mobile. The sight of his sweet face warmed her heart.

Chris stepped up behind her, wrapped his arms around her chest, and whispered, "He'll sleep for another hour."

Wendy spun around and melted into her husband's arms. "Our son is such a happy baby."

"Because he has an amazing mother, who deserves a serious shopping trip." Chris released her, then held her hand as they eased out of the nursery.

They strode to the open-plan kitchen, dining room, and den. "Given I now fit into my regular clothes, it's as if I have a whole new wardrobe. Which means I don't need to spend time or money shopping."

"True." Chris refreshed his coffee. "However, you sold all your jewelry to help pay the back taxes on Eleanor's properties."

Wendy held up her left hand and wiggled her fingers. "I have these gorgeous rings and the diamond earrings you gave me."

"The wife of a successful lawyer needs more than one pair of earrings, which is why I'm taking care of Ryan this morning so you can replenish your jewelry box."

"I don't—"

Chris pressed his finger to her lips. "I've already arranged for the owner of Owl's Nest to bill my credit card for everything you need."

Wendy gazed into his eyes. "What did I do to deserve you?"

"I'm the one who needs to ask you the question." Chris grinned while brushing a blonde hair away from Wendy's cheek. "For now, head on into town, and don't stop shopping until you have enough jewelry to replace everything you sold."

"Are you sure?"

"Positive. Besides, I want a little alone time with our son."

Beyond grateful Chris had adopted Gunter Benson's son as his own child, Wendy patted her husband's cheek, "He loves his amazing daddy."

"Those feelings are mutual." Chris plucked Wendy's keys off the counter. "It's time for you to go on your inaugural shopping spree as a married woman."

"And my last." Wendy pocketed her phone and driver's license, then tossed a wave over her shoulder as she headed to the garage. After backing out and turning her SUV around, she drove down the driveway cut through the woods and turned toward town. She hummed along to a country pop song playing on the radio—a newly acquired taste in music, thanks to Chris.

Wendy braked at a red light and exchanged waves with a woman she'd met at Hilltop Inn's open house. Nine months after she'd moved to Blue Ridge, she already knew more people than she'd known in Gulfport. The light changed. Wendy turned onto East Main Street and pulled into a vacant parking space. Other than a few maternity outfits, she hadn't shopped for herself since the day she met Amanda and Erica. The same day her credit card was declined because the scumbag she thought was her husband hadn't paid the bill in months. Wendy dismissed the memory, then climbed out and headed straight to Owl's Nest.

Jennifer, the owner—who had also attended the open house—stepped from behind the counter. "Every day customers come into our store raving about your inn."

Wendy smiled at the pretty woman who had also become a friend. "I always tell the ladies about Owl's Nest being the best place to shop."

Jennifer's face beamed. "How's baby Ryan?"

"He's amazing." Wendy fingered a display. "I need a few pair of earrings and maybe a necklace and two bracelets." She chuckled as reality struck home. A year ago, she would have bought dozens of items and still wanted more. Funny how functioning as Awesam's chief financial officer had changed her perspective. She lifted a pair of hoop earrings off the display. Or was it the contentment she felt as Chris's wife and Ryan's mother that cured her out-of-control shopaholic habit?

The owner stepped away to help another customer.

Wendy pulled her pinging phone from her pocket and read the text from her teenaged half-sister. "Harper's driving me to your house. ETA two o'clock." She responded with a thumb-up, then pocketed her phone. Although they texted frequently, Kayla's friend had only driven her to Blue Ridge one time. Why the last-minute visit? Was something wrong? She dismissed the questions and continued shopping.

After selecting four pairs of earrings, two necklaces, and one bracelet, Wendy headed straight to the Sweet Shoppe. Would Kayla and her friend prefer cookies or cupcakes? She chose four of each then drove home. Duke, their black Lab, greeted her with an enthusiastic tail wag. "Did you miss me?"

Chris cradled his son while settling on the brown leather sofa facing the stone fireplace that stretched to the top of the vaulted ceiling. He glanced over his shoulder. "Are you asking me or Duke?"

"Both."

"The answer's yes from both of us. Did you buy enough to fill your jewelry box?"

"I made a dent." Wendy placed her purchases on the kitchen counter. "Kayla's on her way here from Nashville."

"Did she say why?"

Wendy settled beside them and touched her son's foot. "Uh-uh."

"Well, at least I'll finally meet our baby's secret aunt."

"I doubt he'll ever meet either of his biological grandparents."

"There's always hope."

"A thimbleful at most." Wendy released a sigh. "Which doesn't matter much, since he has our two families to love on him."

"Speaking of families, have you heard anything more about Millie's house?"

Wendy shook her head. "She and Amanda plan to head over there this afternoon. Hopefully, the damage isn't too bad."

Baby Ryan whimpered.

"If I'm not mistaken, that's our little guy's 'I'm hungry' cry, which means it's time for his beautiful mother to take over." Chris placed Ryan in Wendy's arms. "I'll be in our office if you need me."

After feeding their son, Wendy laid him in his crib. "Sleep tight, little prince." She pulled the door ajar. Determined to stay busy until Kayla arrived, she walked across the hall to their office and opened her laptop. An hour after Wendy logged onto her online course, a car pulling up the driveway perked Duke's ears. "They're here." She logged off. Her pulse accelerated as she rushed from the office and opened the front door.

Kayla climbed from the passenger side, then rounded the front of the car. Her friend remained behind the wheel.

Wendy peered beyond Kayla. "Isn't Harper coming in?"

"Maybe after she goes shopping." As Harper backed out and headed down the driveway, Kayla stepped onto the porch and handed Wendy a gift bag. "I brought my secret nephew a present."

"How sweet." Wendy embraced then released her half-sister.

Duke sniffed Kayla.

She patted the dog's head, triggering a tail wag.

Chris joined them. "You've met the canine member of our family." He extended his hand. "I'm Chris."

Kayla tilted her head. "You're the lawyer."

Chris grinned. "The law is my day job. My most important role is Wendy's husband and Ryan's dad."

"Wendy's texted me lots of pictures of you and Ryan."

"Come on in and meet your nephew in person."

Wendy linked arms with Kayla and led her to the nursery. "Yay. He's awake." She lifted Ryan from his crib.

"Hi, baby Ryan." Kayla removed a stuffed panda from the bag and placed it in the crib. "From your aunt."

"Do you want to hold him?"

"Okay."

Wendy placed him in Kayla's arms.

"Hi there, little guy."

Ryan gurgled.

Kayla smiled. "He likes me."

"Of course, he does."

"I uhm..." Kayla faced Wendy. "need to talk to you."

Wendy's brow pinched. "Is everything okay?"

Kayla shook her head.

"Why don't you two go out to the deck." Chris gathered Ryan in his arms. "I'll take care of our little guy."

"Thank you, darling." Wendy escorted her sister through the main room and out to the deck.

Kayla leaned on the railing facing the wooded backyard. "It's nice here."

Wendy sidled beside her. Should she probe or wait? "A stream runs through the back of the property. A lot of deer make their home in these woods."

"Any bears?"

Why was she stalling? "Could be. Although I haven't seen any."

Kayla picked at her fingernail. "I think something's wrong with Mom. She's arguing with Dad a lot, and lately she forgets stuff. Important stuff."

The same way she had forgotten about her firstborn child then refused to acknowledge her existence. Wendy blinked. "Maybe she's overwhelmed."

"With what? Except for singing with Dad's band at their bar a few times a month, she doesn't work. Our housekeeper comes once a week, so Mom doesn't have much to do at home, and Dad does most of the cooking."

"If she doesn't have much to keep her busy, maybe she's bored."

"During the past few months, Mom's also had a lot of bad headaches."

Wendy's throat constricted. Something other than boredom was happening. "Has she had a physical recently?"

"I don't think she's ever had one." Kayla spun around. "Mom has a thing about going to doctors."

"Have you talked to your dad?"

"He says she's going through a phase. Maybe so, except for the headaches. I don't know what to do."

Wendy slid her arm around Kayla's trembling shoulders. "What does your heart tell you?"

"I should talk to her?"

"Are you asking me or telling me?"

Kayla shrugged. "Mom's not easy to talk to."

"Because you're fourteen and she's an adult."

"I'm almost fifteen and how come I can talk to you?"

"We're sisters, and I'm only nine years older than you." Wendy squeezed Kayla's shoulder. "When you return home today—"

"I'm spending the night at Harper's."

"All right, when you go home tomorrow, you need to share your concerns with her."

"Can I call you after I talk to her?"

"Of course."

Kayla drew in a deep breath then slowly released it. "Okay then, I'll try."

"Good. Now what do you say we indulge on cookies and cupcakes."

"Yum."

Wendy struggled to control her emotions while they walked back inside. Was her half-sister overreacting, or was something seriously wrong with her mother?

Chapter 4

Two days after the fire, Amanda stood beside Millie under the sunlight filtering through her backyard trees. The acrid odor of charred wood hung heavy in the air. Holes that once served as windows opened to the blackened kitchen and adjacent bedroom. A blue tarp covered the caved-in section of the roof. "At least the brick walls are still standing."

Millie brushed her fingers through her hair. "I'm not about to wait for the cleanup crew to show up before going inside."

"If you ask me—"

"I'm not. Besides, the fire chief says it's safe." Hilltop's chef scoffed as she peered over her shoulder and headed toward the garage. "Are you coming with me or staying out here?"

No way she'd let Millie go in alone. "I'm right behind you." Amanda caught up with her on the front porch.

Millie gripped the front doorknob. "Here goes." She pushed the door open and eased into the foyer. "Will the smoke smell ever go away?"

"With enough cleanup, definitely."

The carpet squished beneath Millie's feet as she stepped into the living room. Soot blackened the walls and furniture. "Nothing in here looks salvageable."

Hoping to inject Millie with some hope, Amanda moved beside her. "I had the same impression the first day Wendy, Erica, and I walked into

Eleanor's abandoned house. Turns out we saved every piece of furniture in her living room except the sofa."

"You were dealing with a little rain blowing through a broken window, not tons of water and foam soaking everything in sight." Millie lifted a vase off an end table. "This belonged to my mother."

"A good cleaning will do wonders." Amanda stepped over to an ornate coffee table with a glass inlay. "This piece is salvageable. So are most of the accessories in this room." She pointed to the bookcase. "Unfortunately, your books didn't fare so well."

"Neither did my sofa and chairs." Millie released a heavy sigh then spun around and headed down the hall to the last room on the right. Amanda hurried to catch up. Millie opened the door and stepped inside. "This is the master bedroom Rupert and I shared almost the entire time we were married. Now I sleep in here with my cats. My husband was a good man despite his grumpy disposition."

Amanda followed her into the pristine space, devoid of soot and water. The subtle vanilla scent wafting from an array of candles on the dresser mingled with the lingering odor of smoke. "He was married to a good woman."

"Even a cantankerous one?"

"We all have our moments."

"I admit I have more than most." Millie eased to a nightstand and pulled the bottom drawer open. "On a whim, I moved Eleanor's journals from the living room to this drawer a month ago." She collapsed onto the bed. "My photo albums are in the closet."

Amanda sat beside her and fingered the silky bedspread. "The good news is your memories and irreplaceable treasures are safe."

"If the fire had smoldered before bursting into flames, or if firefighters hadn't shown up so fast—" Millie shuddered. "I could have lost so much more."

Amanda touched her new housemate's arm. "Sometimes the best we can do is count our blessings."

"Which is what you, Erica, and Wendy did after you discovered what Gunter had taken from you. Right?"

"After we recovered from the shock. Now we'll help you do the same. What do you say we pack your clothes and take them straight to our laundry room to wash away the smoke smell?"

"Good idea." Millie pulled a suitcase off her closet floor and filled it to the brim. "I've packed enough to last a couple of days. There's one more thing I need to take to your house." She removed a pistol from her top nightstand drawer and tossed it on top of her clothes.

Amanda stared wide-eyed at the firearm. "Do you keep your gun loaded?"

"Well, yeah." Millie stared at Amanda as if she'd grown a third eye. "How could I stop an intruder with an empty gun?"

"I was just asking."

"First thing I'm gonna do is teach every one of our Awesam partners how to shoot." She added a box of bullets then zipped the suitcase closed and lifted it off the bed. "I'm ready to go back to your house now."

"You carry the journals. I'll pull the suitcase."

Millie huffed. "Even though I'm thirty-plus years older than you, I'm not feeble."

"I was simply offering to help, not make a statement."

"All right then, I'll pull the suitcase, and you carry Eleanor's journals." Millie released the suitcase handle and pulled it into the hall. "In case you haven't noticed, I can work circles around you and Erica."

Amanda swallowed the cutting comment before it rolled off her tongue, then grabbed the journals and followed Hilltop's chef out the front door and down to the street. Millie scurried past the inn and up the driveway as if she intended to prove her ability to outpace her partners. Inside the ranch house, she hauled her suitcase to the laundry room.

After stepping out of her shoes, Amanda set the journals on the kitchen counter then settled beside Erica on the den sofa. "I assume today's Hilltop arrivals are all checked in."

"Good assumption. What's the damage assessment?"

"The kitchen and back bedroom are gutted, and a good-sized portion of the roof is toast." Amanda released a sigh. "I suspect Millie and her cats will remain our houseguests until Christmas and maybe into the new year."

"At least she's doing most of the cooking."

"Which helps make the situation tolerable."

The back door opened followed by footsteps striking the kitchen floor. Abby rushed in, her face beaming. "I have exciting news." She plopped beside Erica. "The crisis center offered me a full-time paid position starting in two weeks."

Erica slid her arm around her daughter's shoulders. "Congratulations, sweetheart."

Amanda leaned forward and peered around Erica. "Way to go, Abby."

"Good news is, they'll let me work around my college courses. Oh, but you'll need to hire someone to take over my job as Hilltop's housekeeper."

"Your mom and I will put the word out right away."

Abby pulled her ringing phone from her pocket. "It's Tommy. He's picking me up in a half hour." She popped up and headed out the sliding-glass door to the backyard.

Amanda faced Erica and stretched her arm across the back of the sofa. "Now what's your opinion about Abby's decision not to go away to college?"

"I admit she made the right choice."

Millie sauntered from the guest room. "Who made the right choice about what?"

Erica explained.

"Well now, I'd say Abby's new job calls for a celebration." Millie settled on one of the club chairs. "What do you say I treat the four of us to dinner out tonight."

"Maybe tomorrow." Erica propped her feet on the coffee table. "Tonight, Abby has a date with Tommy."

"He's a nice young man." Millie crossed one leg over the other. "Since Abby has a full-time job, you should let me take over her position as Awesam's vice president."

"Are you kidding me?" Amanda pulled her arm off the back of the sofa and glared at Hilltop's chef. "No way we're taking her VP role away from her. Besides, wasn't making you a voting partner enough?"

Millie pumped her foot. "Except you didn't give me an official title."

Erica stole a quick glance at Amanda then eyed Millie. "Will you be happy if we come up with an appropriate one?"

"Only if it comes with actual responsibility and isn't just a label."

Amanda stared at Awesam's CEO. Keeping the peace was one thing. Giving their chef more authority was out of the question. She faced Millie. "Erica, Wendy, and I will meet privately to discuss your request."

"When?"

"Tonight." She didn't dare reveal Wendy had invited her and Erica to dinner at her house.

"You think I'm being unreasonable, don't you?"

"We understand, right, Amanda?"

Understand what? That Millie will hound us until we give in to her insane demand?

Abby returned from the backyard with Dusty padding behind her.

Millie's foot stopped pumping. "Working full-time and going to school will keep you plenty busy—"

"Abby's eighteen." Amanda struggled to keep her voice calm. "Believe me, she has more energy than the three of us."

"I'm just saying she might need a break."

"No need to worry about me, Millie. Mom and Amanda are gonna hire a new housekeeper." Abby waved over her shoulder as she walked out of the den.

Amanda stood, hoping Erica would catch her drift. "Tell you what, Millie, we'll leave Hilltop's phone with you while we arrange to meet Wendy."

"You can count on me to handle whatever happens."

"Good." Erica pulled her feet off the coffee table. She followed Amanda down the hall. "You don't want her to know about Wendy inviting us to dinner, do you?"

"Good guess, Sherlock."

Wendy carried Ryan from the nursery to the kitchen "Our little guy is fed and ready for company."

Chris removed four marinated steaks from the fridge moments before the truck pulling up out front perked Duke's ears. "Perfect timing." He rushed to open the front door. "Welcome." He embraced Amanda, then Erica.

Amanda sniffed. "Something smells delicious."

"Marinated filets—thanks to my sister's recipe."

"Our little guy is ready for a Nana snuggle." Wendy placed Ryan in Amanda's arms.

"Hello, sweet boy."

"You ladies visit while Duke and I head out to the deck and start the grill."

Wendy led the way to the sofa. She settled on one side of Amanda, with Erica on the other. "Kayla visited me yesterday. According to her, Cynthia's been acting strange lately." She still couldn't refer to Cynthia as her mother.

Amanda glanced at Wendy. "What would you expect from the woman who abandoned you eighteen years ago and still refuses to acknowledge your existence?"

"I know...except for her frequent headaches—"

Amanda scoffed. "The ones she causes or those inside her head?"

"The latter."

"You're worried about her, aren't you?" Amanda placed Ryan in Erica's arms.

"For Kayla and her brother and sister's sakes, yeah. Enough about her. What's going on with our Awesam partners?"

Erica relayed Abby's news.

Wendy smiled. "Our vice president has come a long way since we all moved to Blue Ridge."

"Which brings us to our newest dilemma." Amanda explained Millie's demand. "Erica believes we should honor her request."

"To keep the peace, I agree." Wendy snapped her fingers. "I have an idea." She rushed to their office and grabbed her laptop then returned. "Awesam's a mini corporation, right?"

"What's your point?"

She tapped her keyboard to pull up an organizational chart. "We have a chief executive officer and a chief operating officer." Wendy tapped the screen. "We don't have a chief information officer." She read the job description aloud.

Amanda stared at Wendy. "How could a woman who still has a flip phone possibly manage our computer technology systems—which, by the way, consists of nothing more than three laptops?"

"She couldn't, and I doubt she has any idea what a real CIO does. However, what if we redefine the role to something she is capable of accomplishing?"

"Hmm." Erica's head tilted. "Great idea, Wendy."

Amanda faced Erica. "Given you agree with Wendy and since your job as CEO includes strategic direction and organization, you need to create a job description that will satisfy Millie."

Erica trilled her lips. "I stepped in it, didn't I?"

"Big time."

"All right, Ms. President, I'll do it."

"You also need to present the offer to her."

Erica stroked Ryan's cheek. "Your nana drives a hard bargain."

The baby released a grunt, making it clear he'd made a deposit in his diaper.

Amanda burst out laughing as Wendy lifted Ryan from Erica's arms. "Talk about a clarifying statement."

Chris stepped in from the deck. "Are you ladies ready for a glass of wine?"

"More than ready." Erica nudged Amanda. "In case you're wondering, I really do believe you're a good president."

"Are you buttering me up?"

"Always."

Chapter 5

E rica reread the CIO description she'd tweaked a half dozen times. Satisfied with the results, she carried her laptop from the dining room table to the office and printed a copy. Now all she had to do was present it to Hilltop's chef.

Amanda stepped into the space. "Millie's cleaning up. Our guests raved about her breakfast—"

"Which means she's in a good mood."

"Exactly. I told her you wanted to talk to her."

Erica's brows peaked. "How did you know I'd be ready?"

"Lucky guess. Do you want me to go with you?"

"In this situation, three's a crowd. Especially given how you and Millie irritate the dickens out of each other."

"You're one smart chief executive officer."

"Now you're buttering me up."

"Another good observation, Sherlock."

Erica lifted the document from the printer. "I accepted Mrs. Bennett's invitation to join her for lunch today."

"It's about time you and Tommy's mother meet."

"Both times I reached out to her, she had excuses why she couldn't meet me."

"Maybe it took her a while to come to terms with her son's relationship with Abby."

"I'll find out soon enough." Erica waved over her shoulder while heading to the front door. "Wish me luck." Outside, a cool breeze tousled her hair as she headed across the side yard and onto the inn's front porch. After hesitating for a moment, she unlocked the front door then headed through the foyer and den to the kitchen.

Millie closed the dishwasher and pressed the start button.

"I hear breakfast was a big hit."

"Why would you expect anything less?"

"I wouldn't." Erica climbed onto an island stool. "We've created an official title for you."

Millie sat beside her. "Something important with real responsibilities?"

"You tell me." Erica slid the single sheet of paper to her.

"Chief Information Officer." Millie read the two-paragraph description. "Hmm." She pulled her iPad close and tapped the screen. "This article explains how a CIO is an executive responsible for managing and successfully implementing a company's information and computer technology systems. All you want me to do is keep the board updated on local events and our competition?"

Erica shot Hilltop's chef an incredulous look.

"Don't look so surprised." Millie tapped her fingers on her iPad. "Just because I have a flip phone doesn't mean I don't know how to go surfing on this gizmo."

Erica stifled a chuckle. "You never cease to amaze me."

"Are you complimenting or ridiculing me?"

"Definitely complimenting. About your title, small companies such as Awesam don't have technology systems. However, if we ever do, we'll expand your responsibilities. In the meantime, our board needs to be tuned into everything going on around us."

"Including during breakfast with our guests?"

At least she'd anticipated the question. "We only need to know about...alarming behavior."

"What do you classify as alarming?"

Another question she had anticipated. "Any action putting the partners or our guests at risk."

"Hmph. Does this position come with a pay raise?"

Fortunately, she and Amanda had broached the subject with Wendy. "How about a ten-percent raise beginning in January?"

"You mean if I do a good job?"

Time for a little flattery. "As an important member of our team, you understand how a raise is always dependent on performance."

"Of course, I do, and I accept your offer. When do you want my first official report?"

"How about Monday's meeting?"

"I'll be ready." Millie placed her hand on Erica's arm. "Thank you for trusting me with this new position."

As if I had a choice. "You're welcome. Before I leave, is there anything else I can do for you?"

"Order me business cards with my new title."

"Done." Erica slid off the stool. "I'll see you at home later."

An hour after leaving Millie, Erica walked onto Southern Charm's front porch.

A slender, attractive woman approached. "You're obviously Abby's mother, although you could easily pass as her older sister." She extended her hand. "I'm Aletha Bennett."

"Erica Nelson." She grasped the woman's hand while subtly eyeing her stylish outfit. "It's a pleasure to meet you."

"Have you eaten here before?"

"A couple of times." The hostess seated them beside a window. At least she didn't take them to the table where she, Amanda, and Wendy had lunched the day they met.

Aletha hung her purse on the back of her chair. "I hear you and Abby moved here from Asheville."

"We did."

"My husband and I visited Biltmore two years ago. It's fun to imagine living in such a magnificent home. I'm sorry we missed Hilltop Inn's open house. Unfortunately, I'd caught a doozy of a cold."

"You're welcome to come by any time."

Their waitress arrived to take their orders.

During lunch, they chatted about the inn, the Bennetts' construction company, and life in Blue Ridge. Following her last bite, Aletha pushed her plate aside. "Did you know Tommy is our only child?"

"Being mothers of only children is something you and I have in common."

Aletha leaned back and turned toward the window. "I married my first husband the year after I graduated from high school. We were both too young and immature, which is why our marriage barely lasted two years." She faced Erica. "Tommy's father and I were in our late twenties when we married. Twenty-two years later, we're still together."

"Congratulations." What was she really trying to say?

"Abby is a wonderful girl."

"Thank you, I feel the same about Tommy."

Aletha folded her arms on the table. "Given the failure of my first marriage, I believe our children are too young to be involved in a serious relationship."

How should she respond? With the truth. "Actually, I had the same concern—"

"I hoped you'd agree with me. Now we both need to help our children understand why they should date other people."

Erica's shoulders tensed. If she ignored the comment and changed the subject, she'd avoid a confrontation. At the same time, she couldn't let a falsehood stand. Digging deep to gather her courage, Erica laced her fingers on the table. "I understand your concern, and you're here because you care about your son's future as much as I care about my daughter's."

"I thought you were on my side." Aletha's brows pinched. "Except you're about to say but, aren't you?"

"During the past few weeks, I've come to realize and accept Abby and Tommy are mature young adults who care deeply for each other."

Their waitress returned. Aletha's eyes remained laser focused on Erica as she waved the woman away. "Up to this point, life has been easy for our children."

The woman sitting across the table didn't have a clue about their life. Maybe she should explain how she and Abby had escaped from her abusive father. Or how Gunter's deception broke her daughter's heart and alienated her from her high school friends.

Aletha blinked. "What do you suppose will happen when one or both of our children are confronted with some sort of trauma?"

"They'll figure out how to deal with whatever lies ahead."

Aletha turned her head toward the window. "My husband is on your side."

"My intention isn't to take sides. The truth is we both want what's best for our children. Which means trusting them to make their own decisions."

Aletha's eyes met Erica's. "You're a strong woman."

If she only knew. "You had the courage to share your concerns—" Erica summoned her warmest smile. "Which proves you have enormous strength."

Aletha remained silent for a long moment. "I haven't changed my mind about Tommy and Abby. One day something will happen to prove one of us is right."

Two afternoons after meeting with Aletha, Erica stood on the first tee at the Toccoa Hills golf course and wrapped her fingers around Jan Barkley's club. The leather grip felt comfortable and at the same time more than a little awkward. Would she ever play as well as Jan? Erica stole a glance at Brad leaning on his club under the cloudless sky. Was he picturing his wife standing on the tee? Did he regret giving her the clubs?

Erica's heart pounded against her ribs as she lined up the club and reviewed what Brad had taught her about a proper stroke. Her eyes trained on the target. She swung and sent the ball skidding down the fairway. "Not my best shot." She retrieved her tee from where it landed a foot away. "At least the ball stayed on the fairway."

"By the time you finish nine holes, you'll feel a lot more comfortable with your new clubs." Brad stepped up to the tee and set his ball. He took one practice swing then drove his ball straight down the fairway.

"That's what I'd call a professionally good shot."

"I've had years to practice while you've only had a few weeks."

During the remaining holes, Brad seemed distant. Erica's emotions teetered between guilt for accepting his gift and gratitude for his friendship. After she four-putted the ninth green and logged her worst score, exhaustion consumed her. "Do you mind if we skip the back nine today?"

"I was about to suggest we call it a game."

Their silence during their ride to the clubhouse spoke volumes. An ache formed in the back of Erica's throat. Had they played their last game together? Had a set of golf clubs destroyed their friendship? Torn between begging Brad to take her home and the desire to stay, she remained silent.

They settled on stools at the bar. He ordered a beer. She opted for ginger ale. Afraid to make eye contact, Erica glanced at his image in the mirror opposite their seats.

Minutes passed. The bartender delivered their drinks. Brad took a sip. "You're wondering if I regret giving you my wife's clubs, aren't you?"

Why had she been so obvious? "The question crossed my mind."

"Watching you play with Jan's clubs brought back a lot of memories." He swallowed another sip. "Some were too painful to bear before we became friends."

Erica's pulse pounded in her ears. Why hadn't she rejected the gift and spared him the pain?

"To answer your question, I don't regret giving you my wife's clubs." Brad pivoted toward her. Their eyes met. "I can no longer ignore the feelings I have for you, Erica." His voice was barely above a whisper. "Feelings I never thought I would again experience after losing my wife."

Erica's heart jumped to her throat.

Brad touched her arm. "Even though we both agreed we aren't ready for a serious relationship, I hope we can see each other more than once a week to find out where our relationship goes."

His touch and the way he gazed deep into her eyes released a sensation she'd never experienced. Was she falling in love with him? Unable to summon even a single word, Erica placed her hand over his and nodded.

Chapter 6

E rica climbed onto the inn's front porch sending a squirrel scampering along the railing and springing onto a branch. She glanced at her watch. The final housekeeper candidate was due to arrive in five minutes. A couple walked out the front door pulling their luggage. She greeted them by name. "Thank you for joining us. I hope you enjoyed your visit."

The woman smiled. "These past few days have been among our most pleasurable inn experiences."

"We're honored you chose to spend part of your vacation with us. May I help you with your bags?"

"No thanks. We travel light." Her husband carried both suitcases down the steps.

"Thank you again for your stay. Have a safe trip to your next destination."

A car pulled up the driveway as the couple descended the steps and pulled their luggage down the sidewalk. Moments after they rounded the corner, a woman in her late twenties with blue streaks in her dark hair rushed to the porch.

Erica greeted her at the top of the stairs. "I assume you're Sabrina Delaney."

"Yes, ma'am." She glanced around. "I've read lots of good comments about Hilltop Inn."

"Come on in." Awesam's president unlocked the front door and escorted the candidate to the dining room. "Please have a seat."

Sabrina complied. "How many people have applied for the job?"

Erica sat across from her. "You're the third. My daughter, who's our current housekeeper, has been offered a full-time job at the crisis center."

"I see." Sabrina removed a folded paper from her purse then pushed it across the table. "I brought a resume."

Erica unfolded then scanned the single sheet of paper. "How long have you lived in McCaysville?"

"My whole life."

"You're currently working as a housekeeper at the Hampton Inn. Why are you applying for a different job?"

"The Hampton is a nice place, but it's a hotel. I've always wanted to work in a fancy place. Keeping this inn and all the pretty things clean would be a lot more fun than working in a place where all the rooms are the same and kind of boring."

"I appreciate your interest. However, we have seven rooms and except for emergencies, we only clean after a guest checks out. Our chef would also need your help in the kitchen every morning at seven. Overall, our position requires about four hours a day. However, the days we don't have checkouts, you won't need to show up. What all that means is we couldn't pay as much as I imagine you're earning in your current job."

"I work four nights a week as a waitress, so part-time suits me fine, and I'm always looking for new experiences." Sabrina peered around the room. "This is where your guests come for a gourmet breakfast, right?"

"Yes."

"Even though Hilltop costs more and is a few miles from downtown, I see why people enjoy staying at a luxury inn more than at a cookie-cutter hotel. Especially since this was once a private home."

She had obviously done her homework. "I appreciate your enthusiasm. My partners and I will review our applicants and let you know our decision in a few days."

"If you hire me, I promise to do a good job and show up on time. Some people my age can't go more than ten minutes without checking social media, but I keep my phone in my pocket while I work. I figure whoever's paying me deserves my full attention. Anyway, I'll wait to hear from you."

"Thank you again for coming by." Erica stood and led the way out the front door. After escorting Sabrina to her car, she crossed the side yard to the carport. Inside the kitchen she set the inn key on the counter then strode into the den.

Amanda looked up from her laptop. "How'd the interview go?"

"Sabrina's the youngest and the most likable of the three applicants. The final decision depends on what Chris discovered." Erica settled across from Awesam's president.

Amanda pushed her laptop aside. "How are you feeling twenty-two hours after Brad's revelation?"

Erica shrugged. "Happy? Confused?"

Amanda leaned close. "Sounds like love to me."

"Or a bad case of indigestion."

Millie wandered in, sat between Amanda and Erica, and set her iPad on the table. "What have you two been talking about?"

No way she'd reveal details about yesterday's golf game to their temporary houseguest. Erica tapped the resume. "Today's interview."

Millie's eyes shifted from Erica to Amanda then back to Erica. "Are you sure you weren't talking about something more exciting?"

"Why are you doubting my answer?"

"Because your expression is akin to a happy kitty that finally caught a canary."

"Hmm." Erica's head tilted. "This is the first time I've been compared to a cat."

Millie huffed. "You're not going to tell me what you were really talking about, are you?"

"You're right." Amanda chuckled. "Except instead of a canary, Erica caught a bird she's saving for your kitties."

"You two are hilarious, even if you are keeping secrets from me."

Wendy breezed in the back door with Ryan snuggled to her chest in a baby carrier wrap. She lowered onto a chair beside Millie. "Have I missed anything?"

"Only our chef's suspicious observations." Amanda touched Ryan's bootie-clad foot. "When can I hold my grandson?"

"The moment he wakes up. In the meantime, I have information about our candidates." Wendy removed three sheets of paper from her jeans pocket and set them on the table. "Good news is there's nothing suspicious about any of them. Who do you believe is the best fit, Erica?"

"The young woman I met today seemed the most eager. However, before I decide, I want your opinion." Erica read Sabrina's resume aloud then relayed details about the interview.

Amanda nodded. "She sounds good to me."

"I agree," added Millie.

Wendy signaled a thumbs-up.

"All right then. I'll offer her the job tomorrow."

"Good." Amanda opened her laptop. "Now we need to talk about our December plans. The inn will be closed to the public for a full week. The second night we'll host a party for family and special friends. Kevin's parents and grandmother plan to spend Christmas at the inn, and of course, Morgan and Kevin will be here."

"I'm working on a budget for food and decorations." A coo prompted Wendy to untie her carrier wrap. "Someone is ready for a Nana snuggle." Moments after placing Ryan in Amanda's arms, Wendy pulled her ringing phone from her pocket. Her face paled. "Kayla never calls. She only texts. Something's wrong." Wendy slid her finger across the screen, then pressed the phone to her ear and hastened from the room.

Silence hung heavy.

Erica fidgeted.

Amanda rocked her grandson.

Millie tapped her fingers on the table.

Minutes passed.

Wendy returned and dropped onto her chair. "Cynthia was rushed to the hospital after she collapsed from a seizure. They're running tests to find out what's wrong." Her voice quivered. "Even though she abandoned me and continues to deny my existence, I don't want her to be sick." Tears pooled and tracked down Wendy's cheeks.

Millie scooted her chair close and wrapped her arm around Wendy's shoulders. "Any number of events can trigger a seizure. Most aren't life-threatening."

Erica nodded. "Millie's right. Let's pray for her right now."

Wendy dabbed her cheeks. "Thank you."

After praying, Erica sensed something positive would come from whatever medical challenge Cynthia faced.

Following Awesam's board meeting, Wendy drove straight home and carried her sleeping baby to his crib. Still shaken from Kayla's phone call, she tiptoed from the nursery and collapsed onto the sofa. She kicked off her shoes and propped her feet on the coffee table. Duke crept onto the cushion beside her and plopped his head in her lap. She stroked his head. "Even though you're not allowed to climb onto the furniture, we know you sneak up here every time you're alone."

The sound of the garage door opening sent Duke scrambling off the sofa and racing to the kitchen. A door closing followed by footsteps announced Chris's arrival. He settled beside Wendy. Duke sprawled on the floor. "The cushion's still warm. Either you were lying down, or our naughty dog broke the rules again."

"I didn't shoo him off this time."

Chris chuckled. "My wife, a pushover for a dog. Anything interesting happen at the board meeting?"

"Kayla called." She relayed the conversation. "When I was seven, my foster parent's son collapsed from a seizure. It scared me so much I raced to the room I shared with two other foster kids and hid under my bed. When the boy's mother explained how his brain was wired wrong, I imagined a tangle of wires inside his head."

Chris slid his arm around Wendy's shoulder. "You've suffered more than your share of traumatic experiences."

Wendy picked at her fingernail. "Sometimes I feel guilty for not reaching out to Cynthia after Amanda and I showed up unannounced at her front door a few months ago."

"Attempting to pursue a relationship your mother doesn't want would only frustrate and further alienate you."

"What if something's seriously wrong with her?

"Unless we hear otherwise, we should assume she's fine."

Wendy drew in a deep breath then slowly released the air. "I'll try."

Chris squeezed her shoulder. "Starting now with a well-deserved nap."

She patted his cheek. "Thank you for always making me feel better."

He grinned. "Thank you for being an amazing wife and mother."

Chapter 7

Hoping to change the subject or at least ignore Millie's ramblings, Amanda took a deep breath then carried the last breakfast plates from the inn's dining room to the kitchen. "Tomorrow we'll have a full house again."

Millie scraped crumbs into the disposal. "I'm telling you there's something fishy about the guy who sat at the end of the table. He has shifty eyes. I don't know if the lady I checked in yesterday is his wife or his girlfriend."

Amanda yanked the dishwasher door open. "In case you're wondering, this is why we only allow you check-in duty when we're in a pinch."

"As Awesam's chief information officer, I could've asked questions, but I didn't. You just wait." Millie waggled her finger at Amanda. "Something's gonna come up to prove me right."

Resisting the urge to roll her eyes, Amanda closed the dishwasher and pressed the start button. "When are you meeting the insurance claims person?"

"In fifteen minutes." Millie sprayed cleaner on the counter. "If he shows up on time."

"Considering he's responsible for assessing the damage, I suggest you resist giving the person a scolding if he shows up late."

"Hmph."

"At least try using a little discretion." Amanda flicked her hand over her shoulder as she headed to the door, then made her way through the den and out the French doors to the patio. Two guests sat on one of the wrought-iron benches facing the bronze five-foot-tall, three-tiered fountain holding center stage halfway up the path to the gazebo.

She paused beside the brass plaque dedicating Millie's English country garden to Eleanor Harrington. Despite their chef's irritating behavior, she had become an important member of their team. Amanda resumed walking, passed the three-car garage converted to a spa, and crossed the side yard to the ranch house. Inside, Erica sat on the den sofa with her laptop balanced on her lap. Amanda settled on a club chair. "Millie's suspicion antenna was on overload again."

"Now what did she do?"

Amanda explained. "Enough about our wannabe private investigator. How was your date last night?"

"After dinner we held hands and walked in the park." Erica closed her laptop and set it aside. "The closest we've come to kissing is Brad's peck on my cheek. I can tell he's still deeply in love with his wife."

"He'll always have strong feelings for her, the same way Preston will always hold a special place in my heart." Amanda folded her hands in her lap as the memory of her husband's fatal accident flashed across her mind. "If I ever decide to date again, it'll take time to become intimate with another man."

"Even though Brad has nothing in common with Abby's father or Gunter, I'm still struggling with trust issues. Despite Wendy's troubled past, she's moved on better than both of us."

"The resilience of youth."

"At thirty-eight and forty-four, we're not exactly ancient. Although you are twenty years older than Wendy."

"Which is why I've unofficially adopted her as my second daughter."

"The three of us and our two daughters have definitely formed a unique little family."

Amanda nodded. "One of the few good outcomes from Gunter Benson's deceptions."

Abby bounced in from the hall, her ponytail swaying. "Training for my new job starts today after I finish my housekeeping duties. One more week and I'll turn my job over to Sabrina."

"I have a massage client in half an hour." Erica stood and tucked her laptop under her arm. "I'll walk with you."

Erica looped her arm around her daughter's elbow as they headed out the back door and across the side yard. "Have I told you lately how proud I am of you, sweetheart?"

"Twice last week." Abby grinned. "Tomorrow, Tommy and I are going hiking. You and Mr. Barkley should join us sometime."

"Maybe we will." Halfway across the inn's driveway, Erica released her daughter's arm and opened the spa door.

Abby kissed her mother's cheek. "Have I told you how proud I am of you earning a massage therapist license?"

"You and I have our own mutual admiration society."

"For good reason." Abby waved over her shoulder as she headed to the inn's patio.

Erica stepped inside then checked out the sauna area. Everything seemed to be in order. She crossed the reception area to her massage room. After unlocking the door, she headed to her office and opened her laptop to the inn's website. Today's only guest had scheduled a Swedish massage. Would Janice Williamson be a talkative or a quiet client?

She returned to the work area and skirted the table, then moved to the dark blue accent wall. Erica switched on the subtle lights over the waist-high cabinet anchored to the wall then slid the cabinet door open. Which CD would her client prefer? She opted for her favorite. As the soft background music filled the air, she lit a candle atop the cabinet and breathed in the fresh scent.

"I'm a few minutes early."

Erica spun around and smiled at the petite young woman with long blonde hair pulled into a ponytail. "Come on in, Ms. Williamson."

"You can call me Janice." She moseyed to the massage table. "This is my first trip to Blue Ridge."

Erica pushed the door closed. "We're delighted you chose to stay at Hilltop."

"I reserved the Butterfly Suite because I love butterflies. They're so colorful, don't you think?"

"I do. Let me know when you're ready." Erica stepped into her office and lifted a bottle of lavender oil off the shelf. Massaging chatty clients required more energy than those who preferred quiet.

"I'm ready," Janice called out.

Erica breathed deeply then returned to the massage room. Her client lay face down on the table with the sheet pulled up to her waist. This clearly wasn't her first massage.

"Tomorrow's my twenty-fifth birthday."

"Happy birthday a day early." Erica smoothed massage oil on Janice's back.

"Nice fragrance. How long have you been a massage therapist?"

She's obviously a talker. Erica's fingers pressed the muscle from Janice's shoulder blade to her lower back on the left side of her body. "Since June."

"I'm a cocktail waitress back in Maryland. We stayed in Roanoke the night before we checked in here. Have you always lived in Blue Ridge?"

Hoping to waylay too many questions, Erica kept her responses short. "I moved from Asheville last January."

"A friend of mine visited the Biltmore house several months ago. Maybe next year we'll spend my birthday in Asheville. Have you ever been to Maryland?"

Erica moved her fingers to the right side of Jennifer's back. "I was born in Baltimore."

"No kidding? That's where my fiancé and I live. It's a nice enough city, although it's more dangerous than when I was growing up. Are you married?"

So much for fewer questions. "Divorced."

"My fiancé and I haven't made wedding plans yet. He's a police officer."

Erica cringed as memories from the night she and Abby escaped to a women's shelter raced across her mind at warp speed. Was it possible? Did she dare ask?

"Erica Nelson. Funny, Jack has the same last name as you."

Erica swallowed the bile erupting in her throat. Did the young woman lying on her table know Jack Nelson was fourteen years older than her? Or did she know he had abused at least one wife? Was it possible he'd changed? Did the nasty bruise on Janice's upper arm mean he still used his fists? Erica's hand froze. If Abby ran into her father, would she recognize him after all these years? "Is your fiancé at the inn?"

"Uh-uh. He went looking for a place to work out, which means he'll be gone at least two hours."

During the remainder of the massage, Erica tuned out her client's chatter while struggling to focus. By the time the hour was up, her head throbbed with pain. She slipped into her office to allow Janice time to dress. What were the odds the man she and her daughter escaped from would end up a guest at their inn? Did Jack know she was one of the owners?

"I'm all dressed now."

Erica swallowed against the dryness in her throat and stepped back into the massage room.

"Thank you for a great massage and for listening to me rattle on." Janice handed her a ten-dollar tip.

"Thank you. We're always curious how our guests decided to stay with us. Did you or your fiancé choose Hilltop?"

"Jack was too busy working, so I planned this entire trip."

One question answered. "How long are you staying with us?"

"Two more nights. Today after Jack comes back, I'm going downtown to shop. There are so many fun stores in Blue Ridge. Tomorrow we'll ride the train."

"I hope you enjoy the rest of your stay."

"Thanks, we will."

The moment the young woman with a bruised arm spun away and walked out, a fist-sized knot gripped Erica's gut. After blowing out the candle flame, turning off the CD, and locking the massage room door, she hastened to the ranch house kitchen and downed two pain pills. How should she deal with the moral dilemma playing havoc with her emotions? Drawing on her position as Awesam's CEO, she made an executive decision. After making one phone call and sending two texts, she headed to her bedroom to plan her approach.

An hour and a half after returning to the ranch house, Erica settled on a club chair. She crossed one leg over the other and faced Awesam's president, chief financial officer, and chief information officer gathered on the den's sofa. "Thank you for agreeing to meet on such short notice."

Amanda nestled between Wendy and Millie. "This is the first time you've called an emergency board meeting."

Wendy leaned back. "Chris's mom was visiting, so she's watching our little guy."

Millie eyed Erica. "Did you already fire our new housekeeper, or is this about our suspicious guest?"

Amanda scoffed. "I didn't say a word to Erica about the ridiculous comments you made this morning."

"Well, maybe you should have."

Wendy's eyes narrowed. "What suspicions are you talking about?"

Erica's chest tightened as Millie rattled on about her breakfast observations. Had calling this meeting been a huge mistake? Should she have summoned the courage to solve her dilemma without involving her partners?

"First of all—" Wendy leaned forward and peered around Amanda. "Until we give Erica the chance to tell us what's going on, we have no idea if this meeting has anything to do with our guest."

"Wendy's right." Amanda folded her arms across her chest. "You have the floor, Ms. CEO."

Erica hesitated. Offering some sort of lame excuse for arranging this meeting would create a whole new set of suspicions. She'd set this up, so she had to follow through. "The reason I want to meet with all of you...is because I discovered something disturbing about the woman I massaged this morning. Her name's Janice—"

Millie waggled her finger at Amanda. "I told you there was something suspicious about the guy she checked in with." She faced Erica. "You found out those two are some sort of criminals, didn't you? Maybe they're a modern-day version of Bonnie and Clyde."

Amanda uncrossed her arms and thumped Millie's arm. "Stop being ridiculous—"

Millie tapped her foot on the floor. "At least admit I was right."

"All right." Amanda rolled her eyes. "You were right. Now hush and try to listen to why Erica called this meeting."

"Hmph."

Sweat invaded the back of Erica's neck. "Janice is here from Baltimore with her fiancé. His name is Jack Nelson."

Wendy gasped.

Amanda's jaw dropped.

Millie's eyes widened as if the light had suddenly come on. "Jack is Abby's father, isn't he?"

Erica nodded. "The man my daughter feared would kill me. Which is why I'm caught in a moral dilemma between treating him and his fiancée as guests, and warning Janice she's engaged to an abusive man. Then there's Abby. If she runs into him and recognizes him, will he traumatize her all over again?"

Wendy's head tilted. "Is it possible your ex has changed?"

"All I know is Janice had a nasty bruise on her arm which could have come from a fist." Erica's shoulders slumped. "The main reason I called this meeting is because I need your help deciding what to do."

Millie's eyes narrowed. "If you were Janice, wouldn't you want someone to warn you?"

Wendy held up a finger. "Except if Jack did give her a bruise, she already knows he's abusive."

Millie shrugged. "I still say Erica needs to warn her."

Hoping for a logical response, Erica eyed Amanda. "As Awesam's president, what's your opinion?"

"We definitely have a problem on our hands." Amanda released a heavy sigh. "Since Jack and Jennifer are Hilltop guests, we need to tread lightly."

Millie scoffed. "Namby-pamby approaches are why men get away with abusing women. I say we confront the monster and save Janice from a miserable marriage."

Amanda crossed her legs and pumped her foot. "Exactly how do you suggest Erica should confront her ex?"

"I have an idea." Wendy faced Amanda. "You and Erica both help Millie serve breakfast when we have a full house. If Erica didn't know Jack was a guest, she'd show up tomorrow morning, right?"

"True."

"There you go." Wendy's focus shifted to Erica. "Stick to your normal routine and let Jack's response guide you."

"Not a bad idea." Amanda's foot stilled. "Okay, I agree with Wendy."

"So do I," added Millie.

Erica trilled her lips. "What about Abby?"

"Your daughter is a confident young woman. In my opinion, you should tell her what's going on and trust her to decide how to best react to the situation."

Chapter 8

Seven hours after the emergency board meeting ended, Erica continued to waffle between accepting and ignoring her partners' recommendation. She glanced at her watch for the umpteenth time, then headed down the hall to her daughter's empty room. Dusty followed her and stretched out on the floor beside the beanbag chair. Erica stepped inside, grabbed the teddy bear, and fingered the pink ribbon. If she decided not to bring her daughter into the loop, wasn't that tantamount to treating her as if she were still a child? Did she dare risk Abby running into her father by accident?

Dusty sprang to her feet and bolted from the room, making it clear she had less than a minute to decide her next move.

Abby breezed in followed by her canine companion. "Hey, Mom. What's up?"

Decision time. Drawing in a deep breath, Erica tossed the bear on the bed then released the air. "Close the door, sweetheart. We need to talk."

"Uh-oh. Am I in trouble?"

"Hardly."

Abby pushed the door closed then plopped onto the twin bed beside her bear. "What's going on?"

"Something happened today you need to know about." Erica sat beside her daughter.

Abby's brows gathered in. "Did you break up with Mr. Barkley?"

Erica shook her head. "What I'm about to tell you will stir up a lot of unpleasant memories from our past." She relayed Janice's revelation and the board's recommendation. "I didn't want to make a decision without your input."

Abby lifted her bear off the bed and hugged it to her chest. "Does he know we're here?"

"His fiancée chose Hilltop, so I doubt he has a clue."

A faraway look clouded Abby's eyes as she rested her chin on the bear's head. "That night before my birthday, he yelled so loud he woke me up. I crawled out of bed and tiptoed down the hall. When I peeked into the living room—" Her voice cracked. "He hit you so hard. I wanted to rush in and beg him to stop, but I was too frightened to move. Then the next day when you asked me what I'd wished for when I blew out my birthday candles..."

Guilt consumed Erica as she wrapped her arm around Abby's shoulders and pulled her close. "Your bravery gave me the courage to do what I should have done the first time he hit me."

"They're not staying next door by accident, Mom."

"Janice has no idea I was married to her fiancé."

"I understand, but think about this. Why of all the tourist towns between here and Baltimore, did she randomly choose Blue Ridge? And why Hilltop Inn?" Abby set her bear aside. "Because my father needs to know you and I are no longer afraid of him, and we aren't victims. Which is also why I plan to help you and Millie serve breakfast tomorrow morning."

Erica reached for her daughter's hand. "I'm not sure him seeing you is a good idea, sweetheart. We have no idea how he'll react."

"It doesn't matter." Abby clasped her hand over Erica's. "You and I are survivors. He can't hurt us anymore."

Erica swallowed the fist-sized lump in her throat. "You're a brave young woman. Which is why tomorrow morning, we'll face him together."

"I love you, Mom."

"I love you too, sweetheart. Now we both need a good night's sleep so we can face tomorrow as two strong and confident women." Erica kissed her daughter's cheek then walked out and headed straight to her room.

Before the sun crept over the horizon, Erica's phone alarm roused her from a restless sleep riddled with snippets from her marriage to Jack. If she had left him the first time he hit her, she would have shielded her daughter from the truth about her father. But she didn't, and now thanks to Abby's courage, they were two hours away from facing him for the first time since they had escaped to the women's shelter all those years ago.

Erica filled her lungs and slowly released the air, then climbed out of bed. She traipsed across the hall to the bathroom, turned on the shower, and peeled out of her pajamas. The moment steam fogged the mirror, she stepped into the tub. How many times during her first marriage had she slid into a tub filled with hot water to ease the physical and mental pain inflicted by Jack's fists? Did he have even a smidgen of remorse or regret over losing his daughter? How would Janice react when they confronted her fiancé? She'd find out soon enough.

After scrubbing her skin and washing her hair, Erica stepped out of the tub. Today when she faced the man who abused her, she would come across as a successful and confident woman. After drying her hair and applying makeup, Erica returned to her room and chose an outfit better suited for a business meeting than breakfast duty.

Following a knock, the door eased open. Abby stepped in. Her choice of clothes made it clear they were on the same wavelength. "Jack has no idea what's about to happen."

Erica stared at her daughter. Would calling her father by his name make it easier for Abby to face him? "I've never heard you refer to your father as Jack."

Abby shrugged. "It seems more appropriate than calling him Dad. When I told Tommy what's going on, he wanted to come over and protect me. I assured him you and I can handle the situation on our own. Anyway, I'm ready."

"So am I, sweetheart." Erica linked arms with her daughter as they made their way out the front door and across the side yard to the inn's front porch. She unlocked the front door, then stepped into the foyer and scanned the living room and the dining room beyond. Millie set two coffee carafes on the dining room sideboard. Relieved no guests had shown up yet, she and Abby followed Millie into the kitchen. "What are you serving this morning?"

"Frittata and hashbrowns."

Abby climbed onto a stool and pointed to fourteen plates Amanda lined up on the island. "What happened to serving breakfast family style?"

"Wendy calculated costs. Plated servings are more cost-efficient and easier to serve."

"That makes sense."

Amanda stood across from Abby. "Today's a big day for you and your mother."

Abby shrugged. "Me facing Jack is kind the same as you, Mom, and Wendy standing up to Gunter in the Las Vegas courtroom."

Millie spun away from the counter and slapped her gun on the island. "Now I'm prepared."

Erica gawked at the firearm. "You can't take a gun into our dining room."

"I don't intend to."

"Then why did you bring it here?"

"Your ex is a cop. Cops carry guns."

"For goodness sake, Millie. Jack's off duty, and he's not crazy enough to do something stupid."

Their chef propped her hands on her hips. "How do you know?"

"Because—" Abby tapped her finger on the counter. "Men who hit defenseless women are cowards."

Amanda nodded. "Abby's right. Look, we appreciate your concern for our safety, Millie. At the same time, we can't risk a guest coming in here and seeing a firearm." Amanda placed the gun back in the drawer.

"Seems I'm outnumbered again." Millie huffed then lowered her hands to her side. "Now we need to decide who's going to serve Jack's breakfast."

Abby held her hand up. "I will."

Erica faced her daughter. "Maybe we should let Millie serve him—"

"The only way he'll know I'm not afraid of him is if I face him head-on."

Erica released a heavy sigh. "All right, but only after he sees me."

"Fair enough."

"Good. Now here's how we'll confront Jack." After Erica summarized her plan, she and Amanda set the dining room table while Abby scooped blueberry-laced yogurt into fourteen fruit dishes.

During the next hour, they debated how Jack and Janice might react. At eight o'clock, voices drifted in from the dining room. Erica opened the door a crack. Six guests—minus Jack and Janice—gathered around the table. She and Millie welcomed and served their guests. Ten minutes later Abby helped serve six more. Still no sign of Jack.

Erica followed her daughter into the kitchen. "I hope he and Janice aren't skipping breakfast." Five more minutes passed. A familiar voice joined the fray. "He just walked in." Breathing deeply to slow her racing pulse, Erica grasped her daughter's hand. "Are you ready?"

"I am."

"All right then."

Millie prepared two more plates. She handed one to Erica and the other to Abby. "Showtime." She pulled the door open.

Erica stepped into the dining room. Abby followed and stood beside her.

The man who had terrorized them all those years ago sat at the end of the table. He turned in their direction. His jaw dropped. Recognition contorted his features.

As planned, Erica feigned astonishment. "What a surprise. Hello, Jack."

Janice's brows raised. "Do you two know each other?"

"As a matter of fact, we do." Erica set a plate in front of her. "Jack is my ex-husband."

His daughter served him. "Hello, Dad."

Janice gasped. She faced Jack. "Why didn't you tell me you had a wife and daughter?"

"You could explain now, Jack, or better yet—you and Janice meet us here at eleven, and I'll explain." Erica squared her shoulders and headed toward the kitchen. Abby followed.

Millie smiled at the stunned guests. "I'll come back to refresh everyone's coffee." She returned to the kitchen, pushing the door closed behind her. "Based on Jennifer's expression, you two came as quite a shock. I don't know if Jack will have the courage to show up after breakfast, but I can pretty much guarantee his fiancée's curiosity will send her down." She grabbed the coffeepot and headed to the dining room. After refilling the guests' coffee, Millie returned to the kitchen. "They both left."

Chapter 9

Nearly two hours after confronting Jack, Erica sat across the kitchen island from Millie. "You're welcome to stay here and listen, but your gun goes back into a drawer."

"One of these days, you'll be glad I'm a sharpshooter."

"Maybe, but not today."

Amanda refreshed her coffee. "I'll keep our chef company."

Millie spun toward Amanda. "So you can eavesdrop, or because you think I need a babysitter?"

"Ditch the attitude, Millie. We'll stay close by in the event Erica and Abby need us. Safety in numbers so to speak."

Abby picked at a fingernail. "We don't know if either one of them will bother to show up."

"If they do...and if they threaten you—" Millie snapped her fingers. "We need a code word."

Amanda rolled her eyes. "You've been watching too many cop-and-robber television programs."

"Give it a break, you two." Erica slid off her stool. "I wouldn't have invited Jack to meet Abby and me if I had the slightest concern he'd cause us harm."

"Mom's right. Abusers are cowards who act out in private. Never in public."

"All the same." Millie skirted the island and opened the door to the dining room. "This is staying open, so Amanda and I can hear everything going on while you two are in there."

"Suit yourself." Erica grabbed two bottles of water then motioned for Abby to follow her. Inside the dining room, they sat side by side facing the pocket doors opening to the living room. "How are you holding up, sweetheart?"

Abby leaned close. "Actually, I'm kind of glad Amanda and Millie are listening—as witnesses to whatever everyone says."

"I agree." Erica set the bottles on the table. "Which is why I didn't insist they leave."

"You and I are a good team, Mom."

"Indeed, we are." A couple descended the stairs and headed out the front door. "At least two of our guests aren't hanging around to watch the drama."

"Where are Jack and Janice staying?"

"In the Butterfly Suite."

Abby twisted the cap off a water bottle. "What do you suppose happened up there after breakfast?"

Erica nodded toward the living room. "We're about to find out."

Janice dashed down the stairs and marched straight to the dining room—her expression hardened. "Why didn't you tell me yesterday about Jack being your ex?"

Erica craned her neck. "Where is he?"

"In the shower."

"He has no idea you're here, does he?"

Janice shook her head. "He refuses to talk to you and your daughter."

"Abby and I hoped you'd show up."

Janice dropped onto a chair. "You embarrassed me in front of all those people this morning."

"Embarrassing you wasn't our intention." Erica leaned forward and folded her arms on the table. "About yesterday. Imagine my shock when I discovered you were engaged to my daughter's father."

"You could have told me privately." Janice's features softened.

"Would you have believed me?"

Janice shrugged. "Maybe. I don't know."

Erica probed the young woman's bland expression. Somehow she had to find out if the man Janice planned to marry still used his fists. "How long have you known Jack?"

"We met eleven months ago at the bar where I work. He came in with a bunch of his police buddies. After he polished off three beers, he asked for my number. He called me the next day and invited me to dinner. I was always fascinated by cops, so I accepted." Her eyes laser focused on Erica. "I want to know if Jack left you, or if you walked out on him."

"Before I answer, I have a question for you."

"I'm listening."

Erica uncrossed her arms and reached for a water bottle. "How did you end up with a nasty bruise on your arm?"

Janice's eyes narrowed. "Why do you want to know?"

"Did Jack hit you?"

Janice blinked. "Was he a police officer when you married him?"

"He was."

"Then you know he has a stressful job."

Erica's nostrils flared. "How many times has he used his fists to hurt you?"

She fingered her engagement ring. "He always apologizes."

Erica's heart ached for their young guest. "Abusive men always apologize after hitting a woman."

"I didn't say he was abusive."

"Your bruise is all the proof I need." Erica's eyes remained trained on Jack's latest victim. "You planned this entire trip, right?"

Janice nodded.

"The day you reserved a room at our inn could end up being the luckiest day of your young life."

Her brows drew together. "How does you embarrassing me qualify as lucky?"

"I didn't become Jack's punching bag until after we were married for a few months. He started early with you. Now you have the chance to walk away before you're trapped in an abusive marriage."

Janice remained silent for a long moment. "You divorced him, didn't you?"

Erica nodded. "Abby and I fled to a different city so he wouldn't find us. What did he tell you after you left the dining room this morning?"

"He said you ran off with another man and broke his heart when you took his daughter away from him."

Abby drummed her fingers. "Jack lied to you. Mom and I fled to a women's shelter because I was afraid he'd end up hitting her hard enough to kill her."

The color drained from Janice's face.

Jack hauled two suitcases down the stairs seconds before striding to the dining room. He gripped his fiancée's shoulders. "I don't know what ridiculous stories my ex and daughter have told you about me."

Janice twisted away from his grip. "You lied to me."

"To protect you."

"Protect her from what, Jack?" Erica locked eyes with her ex. "The reason why your daughter and I fled our home in the middle of the night and ended up in a women's shelter?"

He glared at her. "You had no right to ambush me at breakfast."

"You sat at our table. We served you along with all our other guests."

"You won't humiliate me tomorrow. We're checking out of this dump today."

Erica's eyes met Janice's. She lowered her voice. "You know the truth. Now's your chance to avoid a terrible mistake."

"Don't listen to them." Jack's eyes narrowed. "We're leaving now."

Janice hesitated. "I'm...not going with you." Her voice quivered.

Jack gripped her shoulders again. "Yes, you are."

Janice attempted to twist away. "You're hurting me."

Awesam's CIO and president walked in from the kitchen and stood behind Erica and Abby. "I suggest you listen to the lady, Mr. Nelson, before we're forced to take action." Millie's tone failed to mask her more-than-subtle threat.

Jack's nostrils flared. His glare at Erica intensified. "You're making a big mistake."

Erica cringed. Was his anger directed toward Janice or toward her?

"You want me to walk out on you?" Jack yanked his hands away from his fiancée's shoulders. "Good luck finding a ride back to Baltimore." He pivoted, then raced across the living room and hauled one suitcase out the front door.

Erica's eyes met Janice's. "You made the right decision."

She blinked as if emerging from a fog. "Did I?" Her voice quivered. "This morning, I was on vacation with my future husband. Now I'm a loser stuck here without a fiancé and without wheels."

"You're a winner, not a loser." Millie scooted around the table and sat beside Janice. "Even better, you're in the company of survivors. After a scumbag stole everything from these ladies, they started a business and sold what they had left to pay the back taxes and bring this once rundown house back to life as an inn." Millie patted the young woman's hand. "You have the same courage inside to walk away from a coward who uses women as his personal punching bags."

Erica stared wide-eyed. Who was this woman who had instantly transformed into a cheerleader?

"Millie's right." Amanda sat on the other side of Janice. "Your life free from a man who doesn't deserve you begins now. We'll help you plan your next moves."

Erica marveled at the scene unfolding across the table. Amanda had envisioned creating a luxury retreat where women were treated with dignity—a place where they could form friendships and heal. Wendy mocked her idea with the tagline, 'if your husband dumps you, come hang out with us, and we'll make you feel all better.' At least for the moment, their president's vision had become a reality.

By noon, Wendy's patience had run out. Four hours after they'd served the inn's guests breakfast, Erica and Amanda still weren't responding to her calls. She'd also failed to reach Abby and Millie. Fearing their confrontation with Jack had gone horribly wrong, she secured Ryan's car carrier in the back seat then backed out of the garage. The closer she came to her destination, the faster her pulse raced.

Wendy drove up the ranch house driveway and parked behind Abby's car. She secured her sleeping child in her baby carrier wrap then stepped into the kitchen. "Is anyone home?"

No response.

She rushed across the side yard to the inn's front porch and unlocked the door. Familiar voices drifted into the foyer. Relieved, Wendy headed straight to the dining room. "I've been dying to find out what happened."

Amanda spun toward her. "Janice, meet Awesam's chief financial officer and mother of my honorary grandson."

"She's another brave survivor," added Millie.

The young woman turned and faced Wendy. "Hi."

"It's nice to meet you." Wendy's eyes skimmed the room. "Where is he?"

"The man I thought I was going to marry?"

"Yeah."

"On his way back to Baltimore."

Millie squeezed Janice's hand. "Our friend sent the bum packing."

Wendy imagined Hilltop's chef rushing in from the kitchen wielding her firearm. "Talk about packing—did you—"

Millie shook her head. "I threatened the coward with words instead of a gun."

Janice's mouth fell open. "If you'd come in here armed...even off duty, Jack straps a pistol to his ankle."

"Oh my gosh." Erica pressed her hand to her throat. "I had totally forgotten about his hidden gun."

Millie drummed her fingers. "Lucky for us, I stashed my pistol in the kitchen drawer."

Amanda's eye roll sent a shiver racing through Wendy. If her partners hadn't insisted their CIO put her gun away, the morning might have ended with a far different outcome.

Chapter 10

After rescuing Janice from a future nightmare, the question lingering beneath the surface broke free and sent a shiver up Erica's spine. Had saving the young woman sitting across the inn's dining room table put her and Abby in danger? Before this morning, Jack had no idea where they lived. Even though he'd agreed to a divorce to protect his career, had his anger intensified to the point of retaliation?

Abby leaned close. "Are you okay, Mom?"

Erica blinked. She couldn't allow her daughter one moment of anxiety. "I'm fine, sweetheart." She tuned into the conversation across the table.

"Then it's settled." Amanda faced Janice "You'll have dinner at our house tonight. Do you want us to bring tomorrow's breakfast to your room?"

She blinked. "How many of today's guests will be here tomorrow?"

"Other than Jack, all except two."

"If I hide out in shame, everyone will pity me as a victim." Janice slid her engagement ring off her finger. "If I show up and explain what happened, they'll know I'm a strong woman with enough self-respect to walk away from an abusive relationship. Tomorrow morning I'll eat breakfast right here."

Amanda gave a thumbs-up. "Good for you."

"I know this is a lot to ask." Jennifer held her ring up to the light. "Is there someplace in town where I can sell this?"

Millie snapped her fingers. "I know the perfect place."

"When Erica, Amanda, and I sold our jewelry to pay the back taxes and take possession of this place, we turned our lives around." Wendy released Ryan from her baby wrap. "Selling your ring will do the same for you."

Jennifer slid the ring into her jeans pocket. "Can we go now?"

"The sooner the better." Amanda stood. "I'll drive while Millie shows us where to go."

Wendy lifted off her chair. "Since everyone's safe, I'll head on home."

After Wendy and the others walked out of the inn, Erica and Abby made their way to the ranch house and collapsed onto the den sofa. Dusty sprawled on the floor at their feet.

"I'm proud of you, sweetheart. You were strong and confident."

"You know what? Every once in a while, I wondered if my father felt any regret about losing us." Abby released a heavy sigh as tears pooled and escaped. "Truth is, he doesn't care anything about me."

Erica wrapped her arm around her child and pulled her close. "Jack isn't capable of caring for anyone other than himself. You're fortunate Tommy is nothing like your father."

"You deserve to have a loving relationship with a good man who adores you, Mom." Abby swiped her fingers across her cheeks. "Where's Mr. Barkley taking you tonight?"

"I don't know."

"Has he kissed you?"

Erica squeezed Abby's shoulder. "There we go, switching roles again."

"Well, has he?"

"Not yet."

"Maybe you should kiss him first."

Erica chuckled. "Thanks for the dating advice, Ms. Twenty-first-century Woman. However, I'm old fashioned enough to wait for him to make the first move."

"Know what? So am I."

After spending another hour chatting about their lives, Abby's phone pinged a text. "Tommy's on the way over." She popped up. "We're going to a movie at the Swan tonight."

Erica followed her daughter and her canine companion to the hall. "A drive-in theater. One more Blue Ridge claim to fame."

"I love this town." Abby waved over her shoulder while heading toward the hall.

Erica headed to her bedroom, closed the door, and slid off her shoes. Physically and emotionally exhausted, she dropped onto her bed and lifted the book she'd begun reading a week ago off her nightstand. Halfway through a chapter, she lost the struggle to keep her eyes open and drifted to sleep.

A ping startled her awake. Erica grabbed her phone. Brad was on his way to pick her up. She bolted out of bed and dashed to the bathroom. After freshening her makeup, she rushed to her room and changed into slacks and a casual pullover sweater. The doorbell rang. Erica spritzed perfume behind her ears then stole a quick glance in the mirror. At least she didn't appear to have just awakened from a deep sleep. She breathed deeply to regain her composure then headed to the foyer

Brad chatted with Amanda.

Erica moved to his side. "As usual, you're right on time."

He smiled. "I hear you pulled off a successful rescue."

"We did." Erica looped her hand around his bicep as he escorted her to his Corvette. "I'll tell you all about it on the way."

Ten minutes later, Brad turned onto a driveway leading to a white single-story house with stone trim centered on a wooded lot. He circled to the passenger side, opened the door, and held out his hand. "Tonight, Jimmy and I are treating you to a Barkley boys' version of a home-cooked meal."

"Sounds intriguing." Erica accepted his hand and climbed out. Her heart beat wildly in her chest while they headed up the sidewalk to the home where Brad and Jan had raised their sons—a home filled with happy and sad memories. The succulent scents of tomatoes and cheese greeted them as they stepped inside. The foyer opened on the right to a tastefully decorated contemporary living and dining room. An array of family photos adorned the white-brick fireplace mantel.

A tall young man who was unmistakenly Brad's son walked in from the den at the end of the foyer.

"Erica, meet my son, Jimmy."

"It's a pleasure to meet you." Erica smiled and extended her hand. "Your dad has spoken highly of you and your brother."

His grip was firm, his eyes sad. "He's also told me nice things about you and Abby." He released her hand.

Brad grinned. "Seems we have a mutual admiration society going on. Come on in the kitchen while we put the final touches on our genuine Italian dinner." He led Erica through the den to the open kitchen. "Lasagna and Caesar salad are our specialties."

Jimmy transferred garlic bread from an oven pan to a platter then carried it to an oval table. "After Mom died, we had to learn how to cook or exist on fast food. Turned out our football coach dad is a pretty good cook."

"By default." After setting individual lasagna servings on the table beside the salad plates, Brad uncorked a bottle of red wine and filled three glasses. He seated Erica on the padded banquette built into the bay window, then slid in beside her. Jimmy sat across the table.

After Brad blessed the meal, Erica tasted the lasagna. "This is delicious."

"The secret is Italian sausage. Jimmy's idea."

"I must say this beats Millie's lasagna by a mile."

Jimmy swallowed a bite. "Who's Millie?"

"Hilltop Inn's chef and Awesam's chief information officer."

During dinner Jimmy focused on his food and only spoke when asked a direct question. By the time they finished eating, Erica sensed Brad's son was either struggling from loss or upset about his dad bringing a woman to their home. She laid her napkin on the table. "Since you guys prepared a fabulous meal, why don't you let me help with the cleanup?"

"No need. Jimmy volunteered, with a little nudging." Brad plucked the wine bottle off the table. "While you and I enjoy another glass of wine." He escorted Erica to a cushioned sofa facing a brick fireplace on a covered deck.

Moonbeams cast a warm glow on the wooded backyard. "What a lovely setting. The perfect spot to enjoy the changing seasons."

"Even in the dead of winter, Jan loved sitting out here." Brad set down the wine bottle then stooped to light a fire. "Tonight is the first time anyone has put this fireplace to use since she passed." He settled beside her—his shoulder inches from hers.

Erica's heart warmed as she breathed in the subtle scent of his cologne. Brad had waited to light the flame for her. "Your son is a nice young man. He seemed a bit distracted during dinner."

"Jimmy's always been a sensitive kid. Losing his girlfriend ripped a huge hole in his heart." Brad topped off his wine. "He's still holding on to the hope she'll come back to him."

"Another young person's heart was broken today, but for a different reason." Erica relayed the breakfast encounter with Janice and Jack then described the aftermath. "As far as we know, Jack drove back to Baltimore."

"You and your partners might have saved his fiancée's life."

"At the very least, we saved her dignity." Eager to change the subject, Erica swirled her wine. "I can imagine bundling up in front of the fire while watching snow turn the world white." A giggle escaped. "Have I told you about the snowman in our freezer?"

Brad chuckled. "No, but I'm intrigued."

Erica described the row of miniature snow people she, Amanda, and Wendy had created on Blue Ridge Inn's front porch the day before they discovered they were all married to the same man. "We used pretzel sticks for their arms and raisins for their eyes. Wendy had never experienced snow, so she saved one little guy. In a way, that snowman is a reminder of how far the three of us have come."

Brad slipped his arm around her shoulders and pulled her close. "You're the only guest I've invited to my home since my sons lost their mother."

Erica leaned into him. How many more firsts would happen before the night ended?

Chapter 11

The gloomy early-morning rain failed to dampen Erica's mood as she stepped out to the carport and opened her umbrella. Last night's firsts replayed in her mind during her dash across the side yard to the inn's front porch. After shaking water from her umbrella, she unlocked the door and stepped into the foyer. A guest she had checked in two days ago sat on the living room sofa leafing through the scrapbook detailing the inn's transformation. "Good morning. I hope you're enjoying your stay."

The woman turned toward Erica. "I must say, this has been one of our most intriguing inn experiences."

Intriguing because of Hilltop's history, or yesterday's breakfast incident?

"We're looking forward to another eventful breakfast."

Erica stifled a laugh. Maybe they should add the Jack and Janice saga to the scrapbook. "Whatever our chef is preparing will be amazing." She followed the freshly brewed coffee aroma to the kitchen. "Good morning, Chef Millie."

She eyed Erica while cracking an egg into a bowl. "You're extra cheery this morning."

Erica shrugged. "I suppose because I had a pleasant conversation with a satisfied guest." She moved her phone from her pocket to the island, then pulled a mug from the cabinet.

"What's the real reason you look as if you've won a million-dollar lottery jackpot?"

So much for subtlety. "What's on the menu this morning?"

Millie huffed. "What is it with everyone answering questions with more questions? You might as well admit you're happy because something happened during last night's date."

Erica filled her mug with coffee. "We enjoyed a casual evening at Brad's home. He made lasagna."

"Homemade or store-bought?"

"Homemade."

Millie shot her an inquisitive look. "How did his lasagna compare to mine?"

Erica swallowed a giggle. "I can honestly say it didn't come close."

"At least he tried." Millie poured the egg mixture into a baking dish. "To answer your question about this morning's menu, I'm serving egg and sausage casserole."

"Sounds delish."

"Would you expect anything else?"

"Not a chance."

Abby sauntered in, yawning. "Has anyone seen Janice this morning?"

"Not yet." Erica climbed onto a stool.

"I hope she doesn't chicken out and skip breakfast." Abby poured a glass of orange juice. "We have a lot going on today."

Erica nodded. "Including Sabrina's first day as Hilltop's housekeeper."

"I wonder how many guests checking out will leave her a tip?" Abby sat beside Erica. "Did you have fun last night?"

"See what I mean?" Millie opened the oven door releasing mouthwatering vanilla and cinnamon aromas then set the pan of cinnamon rolls on the stovetop. "Your daughter also knows it takes more than lasagna to make you this happy on a gloomy morning."

Abby nudged her mother's arm. "What's she talking about?"

"Our chief information officer is overreacting to last night's home-cooked meal at Brad's house."

"There you go, Millie. Mom's happy because she's dating one of the coolest guys in Blue Ridge."

Millie slid the casserole into the oven and closed the door. "Are you aware that your mother didn't come home until way after midnight?"

Erica nearly choked on her coffee. "Have you added the role of house-mother to your official Awesam duties?"

Millie shrugged. "I'm a light sleeper."

Abby smiled at her mother.

Erica winked.

Following a knock, the den door eased open. "Is it okay if I come in?"

Erica motioned to Janice. "Please, join us. How are you feeling this morning?"

"The lady sitting in the living room asked me the same question." Janice closed the door then ambled to the counter. "Maybe I should skip break-fast."

"Nonsense." Millie removed a bowl of cut fruit from the fridge. "Every-one needs to see you as a confident woman who dumped a big-time loser."

Erica shot a sideways glance at her daughter. Had Millie's comment about her father embarrassed or upset her?

Abby swallowed a sip of orange juice. "Last night Tommy and I talked a lot about what happened yesterday morning. Even though I decided to forgive Jack for the way he treated Mom, he doesn't deserve my respect." Abby faced Janice. "In my opinion, Mom, you, and I should walk into the dining room together as three strong women."

Relieved, Erica placed her hand on her daughter's arm. "I'm proud of you, sweetheart."

"Then you agree?"

"I do." Erica turned toward Janice. "However, the final decision belongs to you."

The young woman slid onto a stool on the other side of Abby. "Last night I thought a lot about facing all the other guests. It'll be easier if you two stay with me until I finish saying what I have to say."

"Abby and I won't leave your side until you want us to go."

"All right, then." Jack's ex-fiancée squared her shoulders. "The three of us will go in the dining room as a team."

Millie snapped her fingers. "Good for you. You can count on me to stand as your witness."

Erica scoffed. "This isn't a trial, Millie."

Their chef stared at her as if she didn't have a clue. "Of course, it's a trial. And Jack Nelson is guilty—" Millie blinked. "I'm sorry, Abby—"

"No need to apologize. I can handle the truth about my father."

Millie spooned fruit into individual dishes lined up on a tray. "We greeted our first guest a little more than three months ago, and we've already solved Hilltop's second drama."

Janice's brows raised. "Second?"

Millie nodded. "Eleanor's granddaughter's lawyer husband threatening a lawsuit was the first."

"Did he succeed?"

"No way." Amanda walked into the kitchen. "The Awesam partners outsmarted him."

The corner of Janice's lips quirked up. "The same way we outsmarted Officer Jack Nelson. I'll never date another cop."

"Don't let one bad apple spoil the whole barrel." Millie lifted the tray off the island.

"Good point."

Distant voices drifted in. Erica stepped into the dining room and peered through the opening. One glance at the gathering crowd in the living room told her everything she needed to know. Guests were eager to learn more about yesterday's drama. She returned to the kitchen, closing the door behind her. Ten minutes later the timer buzzed, prompting Millie to remove the casserole from the oven.

Janice fidgeted.

Abby opened the dining room door a crack and peeked in, then pushed the door closed. "The dining room's already full. We should satisfy every-one's curiosity now, before we serve breakfast, but only if Janice is ready."

The young woman eyed Amanda. "Do you want to go with us?"

She shook her head. "I'll stay here with Millie and help her prepare the plates."

Janice drew in a deep breath. "Okay. I'm ready."

"All right, then." Erica eased the door open and stepped into the dining room. "Good morning." Janice and Abby followed her. Conversations stopped. Every guest turned in their direction. "I imagine you're all curious to know what happened after yesterday's breakfast. So, before we serve, our friend wants to say a few words."

All eyes focused on Janice as she inched toward the table. "When I made reservations at Hilltop, I had no idea my life would take such an unexpect-ed turn." She hesitated for a long moment, then pulled her sweater off her shoulder revealing her upper arm. "You see this bruise? This wasn't the first time the man you met yesterday hit me."

Some guests gasped. Others' body language and expressions screamed of shock and anger.

"Every time he apologized and promised he'd never hit me again. I believed him because I wanted to." Janice pulled her sweater over her shoulder. "Until yesterday when my new friends opened my eyes." She glanced at Erica, then Abby. "They helped me find the strength to escape his uncontrollable temper. After he left, I sold my engagement ring." Janice lifted her chin. "Now I'm ready to move on, and I will never allow a man to hit me again."

A female guest's clap unleashed applause and a barrage of compliments. The woman motioned to her. "Come enjoy breakfast with us, dear, and tell us where you're going when you check out." The woman's husband stood and pulled out a chair.

Janice's eyes teared up as she joined her admirers. "My brother is on his way to Blue Ridge to take me back to his home in Greenville. I might end up moving there."

Millie dashed in, carrying two plates. "Despite the rain outside, this room is filled with sunshine this morning."

Erica and Abby scooted to the kitchen and grabbed four more plates. Amanda pitched in to help serve thirteen guests. When they finished, she returned to the kitchen and embraced Erica and Abby. "I'm proud of you both."

"This calls for a celebration—" Millie plated four cinnamon buns. "with the best buns in Georgia."

"You and Mom will have to celebrate without me. I'm heading to the crisis center for the final day of training before my new job begins."

Erica embraced her daughter. "I'm proud of you, sweetheart."

Millie smiled. "So am I."

After feeding Ryan, Wendy laid him in his crib and stroked his cheek until he fell asleep. She tiptoed from the nursery, then headed straight to the kitchen and plucked her phone off the counter. Nine-fifteen. She pressed Erica's number.

Her partner answered. "Hey. You're on speaker with Abby, Amanda, and Millie."

Wendy ambled to the den. "Did Janice show up and face the other guests?"

"Oh, yeah." Erica relayed the events.

"Good for her." Wendy dropped onto the sofa. Duke followed and plopped his head in her lap. "Where is Janice now?"

"Enjoying breakfast with other guests as Hilltop's latest hero."

Wendy patted Duke's head. "Today, Amanda's vision to create a sanctuary for women is a reality."

"One fact is certain." Amanda's tone hinted of humor. "Innkeeping is full of surprises."

"Chris's mom volunteered to babysit tomorrow afternoon, so I can check in new arrivals." Wendy's phone flashed an incoming call. "Kayla's calling. I'll call you back shortly." She pressed FaceTime. "Hey. Where are you?"

"In my room." Kayla paused for a long moment. "Mom came home from the hospital today. Even though Dad says she's fine, I've never seen her look this scared." Kayla's voice quivered. "I think he's trying to protect me and my brother and sister from the truth."

Cold sweat invaded Wendy's upper lip. "Maybe she's tired. Hospitals aren't known as the best places to rest. After a few days, she'll be her old self again."

A sigh escaped. "I hope you're right."

"How's everything going at school?"

"Okay, I guess. I'm kind of dating a guy on our football team."

"Good for you."

"My little sister just walked in. I'll text you later." Kayla ended the call.

Wendy pressed Erica's number.

She answered. "Is everything okay?"

"No." Wendy wiped the sweat from above her lips. "Something's seriously wrong with Cynthia."

Chapter 12

Hoping Wendy was wrong about her mother being ill but afraid she was right, Amanda released a heavy sigh. "I'll never forget the fear on my mother's face the day her doctor told us she had inoperable cancer. For a year she endured chemo and fought a courageous battle. At some point, her fear gave way to accepting reality about her days on earth coming to an end. Her confidence knowing she would soon enter her eternal home brought both of us peace during those final days."

Amanda pictured the shock she'd recognized on Cynthia's face the day she and Wendy showed up at her door eighteen years after she'd abandoned her firstborn child. "Hopefully, Kayla overreacted, and her mother's fine. If not, she and her children will need to draw heavily on faith to keep from falling apart. Anyway, enough about the unknown." She eyed Erica. "I need your opinion on something back at the house."

Millie huffed. "What about my opinion?"

Amanda resisted releasing the comment sitting on the tip of her tongue. "We'll talk after you finish kitchen duty."

"I'm a chef, not a worker bee."

Amanda rolled her eyes. "What I meant to say is we'll talk after you button everything up in our professional kitchen." She looped her arm around Erica's elbow as they strode through Hilltop's den and out the

French doors. "At least we have a few minutes alone before our inquisitive chef shows up."

"Do you really want my opinion?"

Amanda shook her head. "I want to hear the latest news about the Erica and Brad romance."

"In other words, what happened last night?"

"You catch on fast. So, where did he take you?"

They crossed the inn's driveway. "To his house."

"Your first time, right?"

Erica nodded as they headed to the carport.

"How did it feel walking into the home he shared with his wife?"

"Actually, a little less strange than I expected when he pulled onto his driveway. I met his son Jimmy. The two of them had dinner ready." Erica shared tidbits about the evening as they walked through the kitchen and settled on the den sofa.

"Enjoying wine beside an outdoor fireplace is definitely romantic." Amanda stretched her arm across the back of the sofa. "Then what happened?"

"What do you mean?"

"You really are out of practice. To put the question more bluntly, has your relationship moved beyond friendship?"

"You want to know if he kissed me, don't you?"

Amanda's eyes widened. "Well, did he?"

"Twice. And not just a peck on the cheek."

"Definitely romantic. Did Brad also say those three little words every woman wants to hear?"

Erica faced Amanda. "You mean, 'I love to cook'?"

"That's four words, and you know exactly what I'm asking."

A smile spread across Erica's face. "Yes, he told me he loves me."

"There you go." Amanda snapped her fingers. "Before long he'll propose."

"Talk about jumping to conclusions. You're way out there."

"Am I?" Amanda held up a finger. "First, he gave you his wife's golf clubs." Second finger. "Then he invited you to his home." Third finger. "And he introduced you to his son."

"Okay, I see your point."

"Now for the most important question. Do you love him?"

A warm sensation flowed through Erica. Although she had been unable to speak those words to Brad, deep down she knew it was only a matter of time before she found the courage. "With all my heart."

"Oh my gosh." Amanda pressed her hand to her chest. "You finally found your soulmate."

"I'm beginning to believe you're right."

Hilltop's chef dashed in and dropped onto a club chair. "Okay, I'm ready to give you my opinion."

Amanda exchanged glances with Erica.

Millie huffed then waggled her finger at Amanda. "The real reason you raced over here was to find out about Erica's date, right?

Amanda rolled her eyes.

"Don't give me that look. I pay attention, and I've learned how to read your expressions." Millie's eyes shifted to Erica. "I already know you had dinner at Brad's house. What else did you tell Amanda about last night?"

"Nothing much."

"I'm not buying, so spill."

Erica shrugged. "Brad kissed me—"

Millie snapped her fingers. "I knew it. You and movie-star handsome Brad Barkley are in love. When are you two getting married—"

"Whoa, hold on to your chickens, Millie. We've only been dating for a few months."

"You're pushing forty, honey, so you can't afford a long engagement."

"First of all, we're not engaged. And second, considering I'm not planning on having another child, my biological clock is irrelevant."

"I'm guessing you'll be engaged before Christmas. Another wedding in Hilltop's gazebo would be fun."

"If I were you I wouldn't make any serious wagers." Erica stood. "Our new housekeeper is due any minute, so I need to return to the inn."

Millie bolted to her feet. "I'll come with you."

"You don't need to."

"Are you serious?" Millie glared at Erica. "Do you expect me to start working with someone I've never met?"

Erica sighed. "Of course not."

"All right, then. Let's go."

Reluctantly assuming her role to manage Hilltop's staff—especially Millie—Erica linked arms with her as they headed across the side yard. "Don't take this the wrong way, but Sabrina will only have one supervisor."

"You don't need to remind me." Millie rolled her eyes. "I know you're in charge of the staff. However, the board made me responsible for gathering information."

An unfortunate decision.

"Which is exactly what I intend to do." Millie pointed to a car pulling up the driveway. "Is that her?"

Erica nodded. "Until I give you the go-ahead, you're a silent partner."

"Yes, Boss." Her tone screamed of ridicule.

Erica nudged their chef's arm. "Drop the attitude, Millie."

"Hmph."

Sabrina climbed out of her car and dashed to the inn's front sidewalk. She had added purple and pink streaks to her hair's blue streak. "I'm excited about my new job."

Millie opened her mouth and lifted a brow.

Erica shot her a 'don't say a word' look, then faced Sabrina. "Come on in and I'll show you everything you need to know."

Millie remained silent while following them onto the porch and into the foyer.

Erica led their new hire to the desk beside the staircase. "Every morning you'll find a list of vacated rooms to clean and any guest requests. Today, the Bluebell and the Chattahoochee Suites are on the list. Beginning tomorrow, we'll need you in the kitchen by seven." Erica faced Millie. "Go ahead and show Sabrina what you'll need her to do."

"Before we turned this gorgeous house into Hilltop Inn, it belonged to my best friend, Eleanor Harrington." The words escaped in a rush as if Millie had held them on the tip of her tongue for hours. She pointed to the book stand in the living room. "After you finish cleaning, you should read all about the transformation in our scrapbook."

"Thanks for the suggestion. I'm eager to learn all I can about Hilltop."

Millie led the way through the den. "Have you ever worked in a kitchen?"

"As a waitress, sort of."

Erica followed and remained silent as their chef detailed her expectations and answered Sabrina's questions.

When Millie finished, the young woman brushed her fingers through her streaked hair. "You can count on me."

"Excellent." Erica approached. "Are you ready to begin day one as our housekeeper?"

"Ready and able."

"All right, then. You know the drill. Call me when you finish, and I'll check your work." Erica remained in the kitchen while Sabrina dashed up the back staircase.

Millie propped her hands on her hips. "What's with her rainbow-colored hair?"

"It's a new fad."

"If you ask me, painting your hair unnatural colors is more than a little strange."

"Her hair is irrelevant if she does a good job. Besides, we hired her as a worker not a partner."

"All the same, I'll keep a close eye on her."

Erica opened her mouth to respond.

"I know." Millie aimed her palm at Erica. "I'm not her supervisor, so I'll report any alarming behavior to you."

"There's a huge difference between quirky and alarming."

"Trust me. I know how to distinguish one from the other."

Erica's brows raised. *Did she?*

Millie huffed. "Don't give me your 'does she know what I'm talking about' look."

Desperate to avoid a confrontation, Erica spun away and walked out. Maybe she should relinquish her supervisor role to Amanda. Except Awesam's president and their chef would butt heads not unlike two angry bulls fighting for the same territory. The image released a giggle as Erica made her way to her spa office to check her schedule. One massage today. None tomorrow.

An involuntary smile warmed Erica's cheeks as her thoughts drifted to last night. Brad's touch. The words spoken and unspoken. She imagined a future by his side. Enjoying life with a man who adored her. Growing old together. Tonight, she would share her hopes and dreams with Abby.

Eager to make good use of her time, she checked her to-do list. Was Brad task-oriented the same as she, or more into details like Amanda? There was still so much to learn about him. Erica remained busy until her client showed up.

Following the massage, Erica pocketed her phone and headed to the inn's English country garden. Eager for time alone to relish in her thoughts, she sauntered up the central path and stopped beside the bronze fountain. Water cascaded down three tiers and splashed into the round basin. Pennies sparkling beneath the water brought a smile. How many guests had made wishes in their garden? How many of those wishes would come true? One of these days, she'd add her own coin.

Erica continued strolling along the path while admiring the garden intricately designed by Millie. She plucked a leaf off the stone path. Ten months ago, weeds had taken over the backyard. Now the space was worthy of gardening awards—thanks to Millie's vision. At least their chef's endearing qualities balanced her irritating personality traits.

Erica stepped into the pitched-roof gazebo with white wrought-iron panels connecting pillars. The chandelier suspended over a white wrought-iron table and matching chairs added elegance to the elaborate setting. She settled on the built-in bench as memories of Chris and Wendy's wedding floated up. If Millie was right about Brad proposing before Christmas, how would his sons react to their dad marrying another woman? Somehow she'd find a way to win them over.

Erica pulled her pinging phone from her pocket and smiled at Abby's text. "Finishing up. Home in half an hour." She responded with a thumbs-up, then pocketed her phone. A squirrel bounded up the gazebo step and spotted her then scampered back to the path. Twenty more minutes passed before Erica walked out of the gazebo and headed home.

Inside the kitchen, she breathed in the savory aromas. "Are you fixing mac and cheese?"

Millie nodded. "To celebrate Abby's first day on her new job."

"She'll love it." Erica ambled to the den.

Amanda sat at the table tapping her laptop keyboard. "With the exception of Thanksgiving and the day before, every room is reserved through November."

"According to Brad, autumn in North Georgia always draws a crowd."

"Lucky for us. Have you heard from Abby?"

"Twenty-five minutes ago." Erica sat across from Amanda. "She's due home any minute now."

"Morgan called this afternoon." Amanda leaned back. "Kevin's parents are loaning them money for a downpayment on a house."

"Must be nice to have a wealthy and generous family."

Amanda nodded. "The loan simply speeds up the process. They plan to pay back every penny."

"Are they enjoying living in Atlanta?"

"Everything except the crowded highways."

"One more good thing about life in a small town," Millie called out from the kitchen. "Not much traffic."

"Speaking of traffic." Erica glanced at her watch. "Abby should be home by now."

Amanda pushed her laptop aside. "She probably stopped at a store."

"You're right. Have Morgan and Kevin found a house?"

"They've just begun looking." They chatted about starter houses, mortgages, and the issues that new homebuyers faced, then Erica glanced at her watch. Fifteen minutes had passed. Then thirty. "Abby would have called by now." Erica pressed Abby's number. The call went straight to voicemail. She called the crisis center.

"Abby left work more than an hour ago."

She pressed Tommy's number. No response. Needles of fear pricked Erica's skin. "Something's wrong."

Amanda scooted beside her. "Any minute she'll pull into the carport and explain why she's late."

Dusty padded over and laid her head in Erica's lap. Did her daughter's canine companion also sense something was wrong? Twenty-five more minutes passed. Her phone rang. An unknown number. She hesitated then answered and pressed the speaker icon. "Hello?"

"Are you Ms. Nelson?"

Erica swallowed against the dryness in her throat. "I am."

"My name is Deputy Gilmore." He paused as if waiting for the gravity of his announcement to sink in. "I'm afraid there's been an accident."

Chapter 13

Gut-wrenching pain gripped Erica's chest. The officer must have called her by mistake...except he knew her name. Her chin trembled. "I don't understand."

Amanda reached for Erica's hand as she leaned close to the phone. "My name's Amanda, I'm Erica's business partner. Who was in an accident?" Her tone hinted of fear.

"Abby Nelson."

Cold sweat invaded Erica's body. "Please tell me my daughter isn't—" She swallowed the words before they could escape.

"She's alive, Ms. Nelson. EMTs rushed her to the hospital a half hour ago."

Erica froze. Why had the officer waited so long to call? "I have to go to her. I'll be there shortly, Deputy."

Amanda scooped her and Erica's phones off the table. "I'll drive."

Millie rushed in. "You two go ahead. I'll handle any guest issues."

Reality struck Erica as if a fifty-pound sledgehammer had slammed into her chest. If Abby only sustained minor bruises, they wouldn't have rushed her to the hospital. She bolted from her chair.

Amanda raced past her. She grabbed the keys and her purse off the counter then pulled the door open.

Erica rushed out and climbed into the truck's passenger seat. Had Abby blown through a stop sign again? Was another car involved? Was the other driver hurt, or worse? Why hadn't she asked those questions when the deputy called?

Amanda climbed behind the wheel. She punched the hospital address into her phone, then called Wendy and backed down the driveway.

Erica stared out the passenger window unseeing. What sort of injuries had her daughter sustained? After she prayed for God to heal her only child, memories from Abby's childhood bubbled up and slowed her racing heart. She squeezed her eyes shut. If she opened them, would she discover she'd been asleep and trapped in a nightmare?

"We're here."

Erica's eyes popped open. She hadn't been dreaming. Her pulse accelerated.

Amanda parked the truck outside the emergency room.

Erica climbed out and raced inside with Amanda following close behind her.

A woman dressed in hospital scrubs looked up from the desk behind the reception window. "May I help you?"

"My daughter was rushed here by ambulance." Erica's voice trembled. "Her name's Abby Nelson."

The woman tapped a keyboard. "She hasn't been entered into the system, Ms. Nelson. Please have a seat, and I'll find out what's happening."

Tears erupted and tracked down Erica's cheeks. She moved away from the window and collapsed onto a chair. "I don't understand why Abby isn't in the system."

Amanda sat beside her and reached for her hand. "This is a small hospital. The medical staff is busy taking good care of her."

"How could this happen when everything is going so well for Abby?"

"Your daughter is a strong and determined young woman." Amanda pointed to the ceiling. "Plus, she's in God's hands, which guarantees she'll recover from her injuries in no time."

Desperate to believe her partner, Erica breathed deeply to slow her racing heart. "Thank you for being here with me."

"We're family, and we support each other through all the peaks and valleys." Amanda nodded toward the window. "The third member of our exclusive wives club is pulling into a parking spot."

Moments later, Wendy rushed in. "Any news?"

Erica shook her head. "Where's Ryan?"

"With Chris's mom. I prayed the whole time I was driving here." Wendy settled on the other side of Erica. "Abby will be as good as new in no time."

Amanda squeezed Erica's hand. "There you go. Another confirmation."

A door swung open. The woman from behind the glass approached. "Your daughter is in good hands, Ms. Nelson." She eyed Amanda, then Wendy. "Are you relatives?"

"Yes," they responded in unison.

"All right, come with me." The woman led them to a room in the emergency room. The curtains were pulled back revealing a space with two chairs and no bed. "A nurse will be with you shortly."

Erica stepped into the space reeking of disinfectant. She faced Amanda. "Now I understand the pain you experienced the night you received the call about your husband's accident."

"Except for one huge difference." Amanda slid her arm around Erica's trembling shoulders. "Abby will survive."

"Which one of you is Ms. Nelson?"

Erica spun toward a nurse wearing green scrubs. "I am. Where's my daughter?"

"The doctor ordered tests—"

Alarm bells jangled in Erica's head. "What kind of tests?"

"CT scans. A normal procedure following an automobile accident. The doctor will talk to you as soon as he has results."

"Did my daughter explain what happened?"

The nurse hesitated as if debating how to respond. "Not yet."

Had Abby been unable to talk? Bile erupted in Erica's throat. She coughed. Her eyes watered.

The nurse scurried from the room, then returned with a bottle of water and another chair.

Erica uncapped the bottle and swallowed a mouthful. "How long before my daughter is brought back here?"

"A half hour. Maybe longer. I know it's not easy waiting, but I assure you your daughter is in good hands."

Erica stared at the nurse. Had the entire staff been trained to repeat the same phrase to everyone, or only when the patient was seriously hurt?

The nurse pulled her phone from her pocket and checked the screen. "Another patient needs me. I'll check back shortly." She pivoted then walked out.

Erica's shoulders tensed. What patient? Another accident victim? She dropped onto the middle chair.

Wendy settled on one side, Amanda on the other. Amanda pulled her phone from her purse. "Millie texted. She wants to know what we know." She responded, then pocketed her phone.

Erica glanced at the clock on the opposite wall. Six-forty. They should be home celebrating Abby's new job, with Millie's mac and cheese—not waiting for news in an emergency room.

Amanda leaned forward. "I can't wait to hear about my grandson's latest milestones."

Wendy smiled. "Would you believe he can turn over by himself and sit up with a little help, and he smiles all the time."

Grateful for her partners' diversion, Erica did her best to tune into their conversation while keeping a close eye on the clock. Twenty-five more minutes passed while Wendy described Ryan's babbles, and Amanda shared stories of Morgan's first-year accomplishments.

The nurse stepped in and handed each of them a water bottle. "We're still waiting."

Erica stared at her. "Why is it taking so long?"

"Accurately interpreting results takes time."

Erica's back stiffened. Did she know more than she was telling them? Was the doctor reluctant to share bad news? She forced her thoughts into submission. "Thank you for the update."

"You're welcome. Even though we're a small hospital, our doctors are excellent."

A knot gripped Erica's stomach. Was reassuring family members another hospital policy?

The nurse checked her phone then left them alone again.

Amanda slid her arm around Erica's shoulders. "Do you remember how old Abby was when she took her first step?"

Erica blinked. "What?"

"Abby's first step?"

"Oh..." She breathed deeply to slow her racing pulse. "Two weeks after her first birthday."

Five more minutes passed while Amanda and Wendy kept the conversation going.

Moments after Erica polished off a bottle of water, a man and a woman—each wearing white lab coats—entered their space.

Amanda stood.

The female physician's eyes met Erica's. "Ms. Nelson?"

She swallowed the lump in her throat. "Yes."

"I'm Dr. Wells, the on-call ER physician. This is Dr. Kennedy, our resident neurologist. I've called him in to assess your daughter's injuries."

The middle-aged doctor pulled Amanda's chair around and sat facing Erica. "First, I want to assure you your daughter will receive the best possible care."

Cold fingers of fear gripped Erica's spine. "Where is she now?"

"We've moved her to our intensive care unit so she can be closely monitored. Abby is still unconscious, which isn't unusual following a traumatic injury."

Erica stared at the doctor. "What are you trying to tell me?"

He reached for her hand. "Abby sustained an incomplete lumbar spinal-cord injury."

Sweat erupting on the back of Erica's neck dripped down her spine. "What do you mean by 'incomplete'?"

"The cord isn't severed, which with treatment and therapy allows for a more successful long-term outcome."

Wendy leaned forward. "You're giving us good news, right?"

"The best under the circumstances. We'll learn more after Abby regains consciousness."

"Was someone else involved in the accident?" Erica's voice trembled.

Dr. Kennedy turned toward Dr. Wells. She hesitated. "A young man with a broken leg was brought in shortly after your daughter."

Erica's back stiffened. "Do you know his name? Was the accident his fault or my daughter's?"

"I'm sorry, I can't share any more details. If you're ready, you can go to your daughter now."

Wendy stood. "We're Abby's family. Can we go with Erica?"

Dr. Wells nodded. "For a little while."

Following the doctor's directions, they made their way to the ICU. Another nurse led them to Abby, directly across from the nurses station.

Tears erupted and tracked down Erica's cheek as she reached for her child's limp hand. A brace encircled Abby's neck. Oxygen flowed into her nose through thin tubing. A needle protruded from her right arm. Wires attached Abby's chest to monitors beside the bed which blinked and chirped with her vital signs.

The nurse stepped beside Erica. "Don't let all this equipment alarm you. They're our way of closely monitoring your daughter. The good news is her pulse is strong and she's breathing on her own."

Amanda touched Erica's arm. "I'll call Millie and give her an update."

"Wait." Erica grabbed Amanda's arm. "Where's my phone?"

"Right here." Amanda pulled her phone from her purse and handed it over then stepped away.

"I'll call Chris." Wendy followed Amanda.

Erica released Abby's hand and tapped Tommy's number.

He answered.

She moved into the hall and shared everything she knew.

"I'm on my way over."

Erica returned to Abby's side and grasped her hand. How would Tommy react to her injuries? Would he stay by her side, or would he leave?

Amanda returned and reached for Erica's hand.

Wendy stepped back in and eased to the other side of Amanda. "Chris will find out information about the accident. I don't want to leave you. Except I have Ryan's car seat—"

Erica touched Wendy's arm. "I'm glad you've been here with me, but now you need to go take care of your baby."

"Promise to call me when Abby wakes up, no matter how late."

"I promise."

"I love you all so much." Wendy leaned over the railing and stroked Abby's hair. "By the time I come back tomorrow, you'll be wide awake. I'll bring us a box of Sweet Shoppe cupcakes to celebrate. Until then, sweet dreams."

Erica looked for any movement behind Abby's eyelids. Had Wendy's enthusiasm penetrated her unconscious mind? "Tommy's on his way over, sweetheart." Did her eyelids flutter a fraction? "I believe she hears us."

"I'm sure she does." Amanda touched Abby's arm. "Millie and Morgan send their love, honey." She and Erica continued talking to Abby until Tommy rushed in.

He stood on the other side of the bed and stared at Abby then faced Erica. "If I tell her something, will she hear me?"

"We believe she will."

Tommy remained silent for a long moment, then reached over the railing and wrapped his fingers around Abby's hand. "If you can hear me, there's something I need to tell you—" His voice cracked.

Erica laser focused on the young man holding her daughter's hand. Was he about to break her heart? Should she say something or wait?

His eyes reddened. "No matter what happens, I will always love you with all my heart. I want us to spend the rest of our lives together making each other happy."

Erica pressed her hand to her chest. "Abby's blessed to have you in her life, Tommy."

He swiped at the tears pooling in his eyes. "I love her so much."

Abby's eyelids twitched.

"Look. I know she heard me." Tommy leaned over the railing and kissed Abby's forehead. "I'll stay here with you for as long as it takes for you to wake up."

The moment Wendy parked in her garage, Chris rushed out and opened her door. "Any update on Abby?"

"Not yet." Wendy grabbed her phone then stepped out. "The love of Amanda's life was killed by a drunk driver. Now Erica's daughter...what if when Ryan's old enough to drive, someone hits his car?"

"What if's are a waste of energy, angel." Chris wrapped his arms around her. "Besides, our little guy won't sit behind a wheel for sixteen more years." A cry resonated from the back seat. "Either my son is protesting having to wait that long, or he's giving us his 'I'm hungry' signal. Which means he's ready for his mother." Chris lifted Ryan from the car carrier and placed him in Wendy's arms.

She stroked Ryan's cheek. "Your daddy and I will do everything we can to keep you safe." Wendy carried their baby to the den sofa and unbuttoned her blouse. "Have you learned anything about the accident?"

Chris settled beside her. "Not yet." His phone buzzed. "This is the call I've been waiting for." He swiped his finger across the screen then pressed the speaker. "What'd you find out?"

"Abby Nelson's car was t-boned when a car ran a stop sign." Chris's contact provided details about the wreck.

"Has the other driver been identified?"

"Yes." He revealed the name.

Wendy gasped. "I have to call Amanda."

Chapter 14

Hours after Wendy's revelation, exhaustion consumed Amanda. She pulled out of the hospital parking lot and turned toward home. Struggling to keep her eyes open, she turned on the radio and hummed along to tunes while driving the short distance. Her breath caught the moment she pulled into the carport beside the vacant spot where Gunter's birthday gift to Abby should have been parked. Amanda cringed. Morgan was still driving the car he'd given her to celebrate her sixteenth birthday. Would she also become a victim in a serious accident?

Blaming the irrational fear on fatigue, Amanda climbed out, trudged into the kitchen, and dropped the truck keys in the bowl. Dusty padded in with her tail tucked. "You know something's wrong, don't you?" She patted the golden retriever's head.

Millie shuffled in from the den. "Any changes in Abby's condition?"

"Not yet. I'm surprised you're still awake."

"I've been planning and praying."

Amanda grabbed a bottle of water from the fridge. "An interesting combination."

"We need to handle Erica's duties at the inn until Abby's well. Everything except massages. You don't have to worry about managing me; I know the drill. If you want to come with me, you can supervise Sabrina.

Even though she's a little strange—with those hair streaks and all—she can help me serve breakfast. Oh, and I fed Abby's dog."

"Thanks for taking care of Dusty, and I appreciate your suggestions, but I'm too tired to discuss anything about the inn tonight."

"We'll talk tomorrow after breakfast."

"Fine." Amanda waggled her fingers over her shoulder while traipsing through the den. Dusty followed her to her bedroom and looked up at her with sad eyes. She stroked the dog's muzzle. "Do you want to sleep with me until Abby comes home?" Dusty's tail swished. "I'll take your half-hearted tail wag as a yes."

After pulling Dusty's bed across the hall to her room and closing the door, Amanda changed into pajamas and set her alarm for seven-thirty. Worn out both physically and mentally, she collapsed onto her bed.

Hours after drifting into a deep sleep, her alarm and a wet tongue nudged Amanda's eyes open. Dusty's muzzle lay on the bed inches from her face. "Is this how you wake Abby up every morning?" Dusty plopped a paw on the bed. "No more doggie kisses."

Amanda swung her feet to the floor and willed her legs to push her off the bed. "Come on, Dusty. I'll let you out." She plucked her phone off the nightstand. After stopping at the bathroom, she hastened to the den and slid the sliding-glass door open. Dusty plodded out to the backyard. Amanda yawned, then settled at the table and opened her laptop. Time for an executive decision. She pulled up Hilltop's website and tapped her keyboard. Once that was done, Amanda texted Erica. "Any changes?"

"Not yet. Tommy's still here."

"Good for him. I'll come over after we serve breakfast." Amanda laid her phone beside her laptop. Following a quick shower, dressing, and letting Dusty back in, she pocketed her phone and headed across the yard to the inn's front door. Inside, she waved at two guests sitting in the living room, then followed coffee and cinnamon scents through the den to the kitchen. "A couple of early birds are already enjoying coffee."

Millie slid three quiches into the oven. "Have you talked to Erica this morning?"

"We texted. I'll head to the hospital after breakfast. You're right about needing Sabrina to help us serve this morning."

"I manage a professional kitchen, so I know what we need." Millie set the oven timer. "Even though she's a bit much—"

"Morning, ladies." Sabrina bounced in. "I'm here and ready to help."

Millie spun toward their new housekeeper and pointed to her head. "Why did you paint those streaks in your hair?"

"Why not?"

Millie crossed her arms. "Do you always answer a question with another question?"

"I don't know. Sometimes, I guess."

Millie drummed her fingers on her arms. "Are you going to answer my question about your hair color or not?"

Sabrina shrugged. "Because I want to be unique, and I think the colors are pretty."

Amanda stifled a chuckle. "Those are two perfectly good reasons. I'm glad you're here, because we'll need your help serving our guests this morning."

"I've had lots of waitress jobs, so I know what to do. I looked through the inn's scrapbook yesterday." Sabrina faced Amanda. "Y'all fixed this old house up good. I've met you and the dark-haired partner. How come I haven't seen the blonde pregnant lady?"

Amanda moved fruit cups from the cabinet to the island. "Wendy's busy taking care of her baby."

"Did she have a boy or a girl?"

"A boy." How much should she reveal to the woman who was still a stranger and, according to Millie, a bit odd? "Erica's staying at the hospital with her daughter—"

"Is she sick?"

"She was in an automobile accident. Anyway, Wendy will be here this afternoon to welcome our three new guests."

"Enough chitchat." Millie pulled a bowl from the fridge and set it on the island in front of Sabrina. "Scoop yogurt into those fruit cups and set them on the table."

"I'm on it."

Amanda's phone rang with Wendy's ringtone. She stepped into the den and answered. "Any more news?"

"Not yet. Do you still agree we shouldn't tell Erica what we know about the accident until after Abby wakes up?"

A couple walked into the den from the Rainbow Suite. "Hold on, Wendy." Amanda placed her hand over her phone. "Good morning. I hope you're having a pleasant stay."

"Yes, we love this inn and Blue Ridge. We have train reservations for this morning."

"Excellent." Amanda turned away and pressed the phone to her ear. "We should definitely wait."

Two hours after exhaustion had caught up with her, strange voices nudged Erica's eyes open. Where was she? She blinked as reality brought clarity. Across the hospital bed, Tommy's head lay on his arms folded across the railing. Her focus shifted to her daughter's still closed eyes. "Tommy and I are still with you, sweetheart," she whispered.

Abby's boyfriend lifted his head. "Good morning."

"Were you able to sleep any?"

"A little." Tommy reached through the bars and held Abby's hand. "I bet you're hungry for a big slice of pizza and a milkshake."

No response.

Erica yawned, then stood and headed to the ICU nurses station. "Have there been any changes during the last few hours?"

The nurse looked up. "No, however Abby's vital signs are still excellent."

"Then why isn't she waking up?"

"There are any number of logical reasons. None of them serious. Anyway, Dr. Kennedy will come by sometime this morning. He'll explain. When did you last eat?"

"I don't know." Erica pressed her hand to her grumbling stomach. "Sometime yesterday."

"Your daughter needs you to take care of yourself. While the nice young man is with her, you should go have breakfast."

"What if she wakes up when I'm gone and I'm not there?"

"Will you at least let me bring you a cup of coffee?"

"Yes. Thank you." Erica returned to Abby's bed. Tommy's stomach grumbled. "Your body is obviously begging for food."

"I am kind of hungry."

The nurse walked in and handed Erica a paper cup, a stirrer, and packets of sugar and creamer. She faced Tommy. "Can I also bring you a caffeine jolt?"

He pulled his arms off the railing. "I'm not a coffee drinker."

"At least one of you needs to eat breakfast."

"She's right." Erica eyed Tommy. "Why don't you go while I stay here?"

"You sure?"

"Positive."

"Can I bring you something, Ms. Nelson?"

"Some sort of breakfast sandwich."

"Okay." He reached through the railing and stroked Abby's hand. "Your mom will stay here with you while I go grab a bite." He hesitated, then followed the nurse out.

After stirring in sugar and creamer, Erica tasted what barely qualified as coffee. She set the cup on a table, then pulled a chair close to the bed and grasped Abby's hand. "Tommy stayed by your side all night, sweetheart. He obviously impressed the nurses. I remember how brave you were your first day of school..." Erica continued reminiscing about Abby's childhood until Tommy returned.

He handed her a bag. "I brought you a bacon-and-egg biscuit."

"Perfect." Why hadn't she asked him to bring coffee?

Tommy moved across the bed from Erica, reached through the railing, and stroked Abby's hand. "I'm back." His eyes widened. "Look." He pointed to Abby's fluttering eyelids. "Your mom and I are both here with you now."

Erica's heart drummed in her chest.

Her daughter's eyes eased open. "Mom? Tommy?" Her voice was barely above a whisper.

"Welcome back, sweetheart."

A smile lit Tommy's face. "Hey, beautiful."

Abby's brows pinched. "Where am I?"

Erica stroked her child's fingers. "You're in the hospital."

Abby blinked, as if attempting to understand. "Am I sick?"

"No, sweetheart."

The nurse walked in, smiling. "Look who's awake. My name is Jen."

Abby touched her neck brace. "Why is this thing around my neck?"

The nurse moved close to her patient. "Yesterday you were in an accident, and now we're taking good care of you. The brace is to protect your spine."

"I don't remember an accident."

Nurse Jen smiled. "Because God protected you from all the commotion until you were ready to wake up."

Abby's neurologist walked in. "Nurse Jen might be on to something. I'm Dr. Kennedy. How are you feeling?"

Abby winced. "Like a giant truck ran over me."

"I've ordered mild pain medication to take the edge off." The doctor pulled the blanket away from Abby's leg. "I'm going to touch your foot, and I want you to tell me what you feel."

"Why?"

He caught Erica's eye. Was he trying to decide whether to treat Abby as an adult or as a child? "My daughter is a strong young woman."

He nodded. "Good question, Abby. As Nurse Jen explained, you were in an automobile accident and sustained an incomplete spinal cord injury." He relayed the details. "Your reaction to touch is one step toward assessing the damage, so we can determine the best treatment to make you well." His tone was reassuring. "Are you ready?"

"I think so."

"All right. Here goes." He ran his finger along the top of her foot. "Describe what you feel."

"I didn't feel anything."

Erica cringed.

"I'm going to apply more pressure." He repeated the move. "What about now?"

Her brows pinched then released. "I think I felt something."

"Can you describe the feeling?"

"It was like you touched my foot with a feather."

"Good. Now, I want you to wiggle your toes."

Abby pressed her lips together. Her big toe moved a fraction.

"Good job." Dr. Kennedy pulled the blanket over her foot. "We'll be taking you for some tests shortly. In the meantime, I want you to eat something, young lady."

"Is pizza okay?"

Dr. Kennedy chuckled. "The perfect choice."

Tommy snapped his fingers. "I knew you heard your mom and me talking to you." He pulled his phone from his pocket. "Your favorite pizza will soon be on the way."

After raising the bed to a partial sitting position, Dr. Kennedy motioned to Erica.

She followed him to the nurses station. "Feeling you touch her foot is good news, right?"

"Yes, however minimal movement indicates nerve damage."

She probed the doctor's expression. "How much damage?"

"I'll know more after extensive testing. Abby's strong and I'm guessing determined as well."

Erica nodded. "Very."

"Those two qualities mean her outlook for recovery is promising."

Afraid to ask what he meant by 'promising,' Erica returned to her daughter.

Abby's brow pinched. "What did Dr. Kennedy say?"

"He believes you're an impressive young woman, with a bright future."

Abby squeezed her eyes shut. "Yesterday on the way home...I heard a loud sound. Then nothing." She opened her eyes. "Until I heard you and Tommy talking to me. Do you know what happened?"

"Not yet."

"Oh my gosh." Amanda rushed in and stood at the end of the bed. "Look at you, awake and sitting up all perky." She touched Abby's leg. "Morgan and Millie send their love and prayers."

"Thanks." Abby tilted her head to the left as if peering around Amanda. "Mr. Barkley?"

Amanda spun toward Brad.

Erica's heart skipped a beat.

He set a vase of flowers enhanced with a get-well balloon on the cabinet, then eased beside Erica. His eyes trained on Abby. "How are you feeling?"

"Sort of beat up."

"I'm sorry about your accident." Brad's tone hinted of sadness. "Do you mind if I steal your mom away for a little while?"

"Go ahead."

Amanda's pinched expression sent a shiver up Erica's spine. Did her partner know why Brad wanted to talk to her alone? He gripped her elbow and escorted her from the ICU to a bench in the hospital lobby.

"Why couldn't you talk to me outside of Abby's room?"

He stared straight ahead. "How serious are your daughter's injuries?"

Why wouldn't he look her in the eye? "We don't know yet." She relayed Dr. Kennedy's diagnosis.

Brad propped his arms on his knees and bent his head toward the floor. "I've been trying to figure out how to tell you for hours. You know Jimmy's girlfriend broke up with him." He fell silent.

Erica's jaw dropped. "You didn't drag me away from my child to talk about your son's love life, did you?"

"Yesterday she texted him for the first time since they broke up."

Erica's heart pounded against her ribs. "What are you trying to tell me?"

"Jimmy was driving. He blew through a stop sign." Brad raised his head. His reddened eyes met Erica's. "My son crashed into your daughter's car."

An explosive gasp escaped Erica. Overwhelmed by anger at Jimmy's reckless behavior, her feelings for Brad, and uncertainty about Abby's injuries, she bolted to her feet and raced out to the parking lot. How in fewer than twenty-four hours could everything have gone so wrong? She dropped onto a bench, buried her face in her hands, and wept.

Chapter 15

Responding to Duke's perked ears, Wendy rushed to open the front door. "Thank you for coming over, Linda." She embraced Chris's mother.

"I'm always happy to spend time with my grandson, especially since my granddaughter is due to arrive in this world before Christmas."

"How's Allison balancing pregnancy and her practice?"

"She plans to continue taking care of patients until her ninth month."

"A pregnant doc delivering babies is cool." Wendy led the way to the nursery.

"Speaking of doctors, how's Abby?"

"She had more tests this morning. Erica hopes to have results by the end of the day." Wendy lifted Ryan from his crib and placed her son in her mother-in-law's arms. "Grandma is gonna take care of you for a little while."

Linda nuzzled her grandson's neck. "You and I will have fun while your beautiful mommy goes to work." Ryan rewarded her with a smile and a giggle. "He's such a happy baby."

"Because he has an amazing daddy."

"And mommy." Linda followed Wendy to the den.

"Do you mind if I go to the hospital after the new guests check in?"

"Of course not. You take all the time you need, honey."

"Thank you." Wendy plucked her purse off the kitchen counter then headed to the garage. After sliding into her SUV and securing her phone in the carrier, she tapped the screen.

Amanda answered after the third ring.

"Are you with Erica now?"

"I stepped away so we can talk."

Wendy backed her SUV out of the garage. "How's she handling the news about the accident?"

"She's heartbroken, but she's putting on a positive face for Abby."

"Has she told her about Jimmy?"

"Not yet. She's waiting to hear the test results."

"I'll come by in a couple of hours with cupcakes." Wendy turned the car around and headed down the driveway. "Hopefully by then we'll have good news." Ten minutes after turning onto the road fronting their property, Wendy pulled into the ranch house carport. She traipsed across the side yard to the inn's front porch and into the foyer.

A young woman with a rainbow of colors in her hair looked up. "You're Awesam's third partner, aren't you? I recognize you from your picture."

"I am." Wendy ambled toward the young woman sitting on the living room sofa. The inn's scrapbook lay open on her lap. "You must be Sabrina."

"Uh-huh. I've been reading about Hilltop. It's such an interesting story. Especially how this house stood empty for all those years, and then out of the blue, you and your friends ended up owning it."

Wendy shrugged. "We were in the right place at the right time."

"Strange how none of you are from around here." Sabrina closed the scrapbook then returned it to the book stand. "Anyway, I'm glad to meet you."

"Same here. Are the rooms ready for new guests?"

Sabrina nodded. "Millie already inspected them, and I've cleaned all the public spaces. She told me you're married to a good-looking lawyer."

Wendy's brow pinched then released. What other tidbits had their chef blabbed about her? "I need to prepare for our new arrivals." Hoping their new housekeeper would take the hint, she turned and headed straight to the check-in desk.

"Since I finished my work, I'll be on my way."

Grateful the subtle message had worked, Wendy glanced over her shoulder as Sabrina headed to the foyer. "Have a nice day."

"You too." Their new housekeeper hesitated then walked out, closing the door behind her.

Wendy yanked her phone from her pocket and pressed Millie's number. She answered.

"Where are you?"

"The inn's kitchen."

"We need to talk." Wendy pocketed her phone then headed straight to Millie. "Why did you tell our housekeeper I'm married to a lawyer?"

"Don't get all bent out of shape. I simply confirmed what she already knew."

"Blue Ridge is a small town. I suppose a lot of people know Chris and I are married."

"Except Sabrina lives eleven miles away in McCaysville." Millie pushed her iPad aside. "Amanda says I'm overreacting, but I'm telling you there's something peculiar about our new housekeeper. Which is why I plan to keep a close eye on her. Have you heard any more news about Abby?"

"They're still waiting for test results."

"What happened to her is such a shame. Especially since we don't have a lot of bad wrecks around here."

How would Millie react when she learned who caused the accident? The doorbell rang. "Today's first new guests are here." Wendy scooted to the foyer and opened the front door. "Welcome to Hilltop Inn."

Two hours after meeting Sabrina for the first time, Wendy escorted the last new guests to their room. "Please let us know if there's anything we can do to make your stay fabulous." She walked out of the Bluebell Suite and closed the door. Eager to head to the hospital, Wendy rushed to her car. Following a stop at the Sweet Shoppe, she drove to the hospital and headed straight to ICU. Inside the patient room Tommy sat on one side of the bed, Amanda and Erica on the other. Wendy eased beside Tommy and smiled at Abby. "It's exciting to see you awake. I brought cupcakes."

"Sugar and meds." Abby managed a weak grin. "The perfect cure for pain."

Wendy pointed to the balloon-enhanced arrangement. "Who gave you the flowers?"

"Mr. Barkley. He's so nice."

Erica's downcast eyes spoke volumes. Resisting the urge to rush to the other side of the bed and hug her partner, Wendy opened the Sweet Shoppe box and held it in front of Abby. "You choose first."

She lifted a cupcake. "Chocolate lava fudge—one of my favorites."

"I remembered." After passing the box to Tommy, Wendy settled on the chair he had vacated for her.

The nurse walked in, smiling. "It's fun to see a patient and her family enjoying each other." She moved close to Abby. "How's your pain level?"

Abby winced. "Tolerable."

"Let me know if it becomes unbearable." She checked Abby's vitals then walked out.

While chatting with Amanda and Tommy, Wendy kept a close eye on Abby's fidgeting and pinched expression. If she was suffering from increased pain, why didn't she ask for more meds? Wendy's eyes shifted to Erica. She had barely uttered a word during the past hour. When would she tell Abby the truth about her accident?

Amanda stopped talking midsentence the moment Dr. Kennedy walked in.

He stood at the end of the bed. "Ms. Nelson, Abby, do I have your permission to share results with everyone here, or would you prefer privacy?"

Abby lifted her hand. "They're my family. It's okay for them to stay."

Erica nodded. "I agree."

"All right. First, given the severity of your accident, you're a lucky young lady to be alive."

Abby stared at him, then frowned. "How severe are my injuries?"

"Your spinal cord injury may impair your ability to stand or walk."

Erica's face paled.

Dr. Kennedy moved closer to Abby. "Having said that, the sever of the cord was incomplete; therefore you'll need to undergo extensive physical and occupational therapy while your spinal cord attempts to heal."

Tommy stroked Abby's hand while his eyes remained trained on the doctor. "What do you mean by attempts?"

"How well her spinal cord repairs itself is impossible to predict." The doctor reached over the railing and touched his patient's arm. "Although there are no guarantees, your commitment to therapy along with your determination will play an important role in your healing process."

Abby touched her neck brace. "My skin itches like crazy. When can I take this thing off?"

"Is right now soon enough?" He leaned down and removed the brace.

"What a relief." Abby scratched her neck. "Can I go home now?"

"In a few days. We'll talk again tomorrow after your first therapy session. In the meantime, I'm moving you out of ICU."

Wendy's brows lifted. "Moving her is good news, right?"

"Absolutely."

Moments after Dr. Kennedy walked out, Abby lifted her chin. "No matter if it takes a week, a month, or more than a year, I will walk again."

Wendy snapped her fingers. "You go, girl."

Tommy leaned over the railing and kissed Abby's cheek.

Erica's eyes seemed to cloud over. Was she skeptical about her daughter's promise, or was she struggling with how to break the news to her about Jimmy Barkley?

An hour after Abby had been moved to a private room, Erica's tension headache escalated beyond a tolerable level. Desperate for relief, she tiptoed from the room to the nurses station. "Is there any way you could give me something to relieve my headache?"

"Not officially. However, as one mother to another—" The nurse removed a bottle of over-the-counter pain medication from a drawer and set it on the counter. "Take however many you need."

"You're a lifesaver." Erica uncapped the bottle and tapped three pills into her palm then returned to Abby's room and closed the door. Grateful her daughter and Tommy both slept, she washed the pills down with a sip of water.

Desperate for rest, Erica settled on the recliner beside the bed, leaned back, and closed her eyes. Images of her partners' frequent glances before they left played in her mind. They knew Jimmy had caused the accident. Somehow she had to summon the courage to tell Abby before she found out from someone else. Would she ever be able to face Brad without reliving the pain his son had inflicted on her child? As her headache began to ease, mind-numbing exhaustion sent Erica succumbing to sleep for the first time since she'd arrived in the emergency room.

"Mom?"

Abby's voice broke through the fog in Erica's head. Was she dreaming, or had her daughter spoken aloud? She forced her eyes open.

A nurse she hadn't seen before stood on the other side of the bed. "Ms. Evans, a gentleman wishes to speak to you outside the room."

Confusion muddled Erica's brain. Why would someone want to talk to her in private? She raised the recliner to an upright position then stood and forced her feet to carry her from the room. Rendered speechless, she halted halfway to the nurses station.

The man who had captured her heart stood behind his son sitting in a wheelchair. A cast extending from Jimmy's thigh to his foot secured his right leg at a slight bent-knee angle. His pinched expression reflected far more than physical pain.

Brad cleared his throat and pushed the chair closer. "We don't want to apologize to Abby without your permission."

Erica swallowed the fist-sized lump in her throat. "I haven't told her."

"We'll leave if you want to tell her first."

Tommy walked into the hall. "Abby wants to know who you're talking to." He stopped dead in his tracks. His jaw tensed. "You caused the wreck, didn't you?"

Jimmy nodded.

Erica's heart ached for all three men. "The moment the four of us enter her room, she'll know the truth."

Brad touched Erica's arm. "Are you saying you want Jimmy and me to leave?"

Erica breathed deeply to slow her racing pulse. "No, Abby sent Tommy out here, which means she's already curious. There's no reason to delay the inevitable any longer." She spun around then returned to the room and stood at the foot of the bed.

Tommy moved to Abby's right side.

Brad pushed the wheelchair across from Tommy.

Abby stared wide-eyed at Jimmy. "You're the one, aren't you?"

Tears pooled in his eyes and tracked down the young man's cheeks. "I ran a stop sign. I'm so sorry..."

Abby's eyes reddened. She held her open palm through the railing. "Give me your hand."

Jimmy hesitated.

"Please."

He placed his hand on hers.

"Thank you for having the courage to tell me in person." She offered a weak smile. "Do I wish this had never happened? Yes. But it did...and I forgive you. Now, you need to forgive yourself."

Blinking away tears, Erica pressed her palm to her heart. Her child had the strength of character to extend grace to the young man whose careless actions sent her to the hospital and an uncertain future. Overwhelmed, she backed away from the bed and escaped to the hall.

Brad followed her. "I dreaded telling you about Jimmy because I was afraid the truth would destroy our relationship. Your reaction confirmed my fear."

Erica pivoted toward him.

Brad's eyes met hers. "I lost my first love to cancer. Erica, I don't want to lose my second to a senseless accident. I hope you'll forgive Jimmy and come back to me." He placed his hand on her shoulder. "I'll understand if you believe our relationship isn't strong enough to survive this tragedy."

His touch awakened every nerve in her body, releasing a tangle of conflicting emotions. "I need more time."

"I'll wait as long as it takes." He kissed her cheek, then returned to Abby's room. Moments later he pushed his son out the door and down the hall.

Erica breathed deeply to slow her racing pulse then returned to her child's side.

Abby looked up at her. "Is everything okay between you and Mr. Barkley?"

She couldn't lie to her daughter or tell her the truth. "All you need to think about right now is getting well. Right, Tommy?"

"Absolutely."

Chapter 16

The morning after Jimmy confessed, Erica's emotional battle continued to haunt her. Her marriage to Jack had failed because he couldn't control his fists. Her second marriage turned out to be a fraud. She raised her recliner to an upright position. Her eyes drifted to the needle inserted in Abby's arm. Even though her daughter had forgiven Jimmy, how could she continue a relationship with the man whose son's reckless behavior hurt her only child?

Tommy awakened and swung his legs over the side of the bench. He yawned, then lumbered to the bed and leaned on the railing.

Abby's eyes fluttered open. "Is it morning?"

"Uh-huh." Tommy reached for her hand. "How are you feeling?"

"Better than yesterday." Abby raised her bed to a sitting position. "Hey, Mom."

"Good morning, sweetheart."

Nurse Jen strode in. "Today's a big day for my favorite patient."

Tommy released Abby's hand. "What time's her therapy?"

"An hour from now."

"Can we go with her?"

"Therapy requires a patient's total concentration, so it's best if she goes alone—at least the first few times." The nurse replaced an empty bag releasing fluid into the needle inserted in Abby's arm. "Today's session will take at least two hours, which will be the perfect time for you both to take a break."

Tommy ran his fingers through his hair. "I definitely need a shower."

Erica nodded. "So do I."

"I didn't want to say anything—" Abby grinned. "But you're both right."

Grateful for her daughter's humor, Erica stood. "I have to admit I've never looked so forward to changing clothes."

"Believe me, I understand." Nurse Jen waved over her shoulder as the food-service lady arrived. "Breakfast is served." She placed a tray on the table then walked out.

Tommy repositioned the table over the bed.

Abby lifted the lid off her plate releasing bacon scents. "I hope this tastes better than it looks." After eating a strip of bacon and swallowing a mouthful of scrambled eggs, she pushed the tray aside. "When you come back this afternoon, will you bring me a burger, fries, and a vanilla milkshake?"

"A meal of champions?" Erica patted her daughter's leg.

"Bring burgers for you and Tommy too."

The lighthearted conversation eased Erica's anxiety, until an orderly arrived and lifted her child into a wheelchair. She and Tommy followed them into the hall. Abby waggled her fingers over her shoulder as the young man pushed her chair around the corner.

Erica released a sigh. "How are you holding up, Tommy?"

"Good enough." They headed in the opposite direction from Abby. "After she leaves the hospital, do you mind if I drive her to work and to therapy?"

Erica studied Tommy's profile. "What about your job?"

"I work for my dad, so taking time off isn't a problem."

If she told him yes, would she shirk her parental responsibility? "How about we take turns?"

"Fair enough."

They headed out to the parking lot. "You're deeply in love with Abby, aren't you?"

"I love her more than I've ever loved anyone."

"She's blessed to have you in her life, Tommy."

"Not nearly as blessed as I am to have her in my life, Ms. Nelson. It doesn't matter how long it takes for her to recover, and even if she doesn't, I'll be here for her."

Erica's heart warmed as she looped her arm around Tommy's elbow. "I believe it's time for you to drop the formality and call me by my first name." Erica stepped off the curb at the truck. "Time for another big decision. What flavor milkshake to you want me to bring you?"

Tommy opened the door for her. "How about strawberry."

"All right." She climbed in. "I'll see you back here in two hours."

"Yes, ma'am." Tommy closed the door then returned to the sidewalk.

Erica smiled. When did *ma'am* become her first name? She backed out of the parking space and drove straight home. Dusty met her at the kitchen door. "Abby will come home soon."

Amanda rushed in from the den and embraced Erica. "How's our girl?"

"Better than her mother." She trudged through the den to Abby's room. "I have no idea what she will and won't be able to do by herself. You know how independent she is. It's bad enough that she won't be able to drive. How will she react if she can't get in and out of bed—" Erica pointed to the door leading to Abby's private bathroom. "—or the shower on her own?"

Amanda leaned on the doorframe. "I read all about occupational therapy. It's amazing what patients can learn to do on their own. Especially when they're young and strong like Abby."

Erica glanced at her daughter's teddy bear poised on her bed. "After she comes home, Tommy wants to drive her to work and to therapy."

"An eighteen-year-old girl would consider a boyfriend driving her a normal part of their relationship. Her mom, not so much. Besides, helping her in and out of his car will be a lot easier than lifting her into the truck."

"I suppose you're right. Although, I still want to drive some of the time. For now, I need a hot shower." Erica headed to the bathroom she shared with Amanda and Millie. She closed the door and turned on the water then leaned close to the mirror. A little concealer would help hide the circles under her eyes. Steam filled the small space. Erica stepped into the tub. The hot water flowing down her body helped ease her aching muscles. Would therapy cause her child agony? If she ended her relationship with Brad, would she be adding guilt to her daughter's pain?

After showering, Erica dried her hair and traipsed across the hall to her room. Desperate for a nap, yet afraid she'd fall into a deep sleep, she opened her closet. The doorbell rang. Counting on Amanda to respond, Erica pulled out a pair of jeans and a pullover sweater.

Following a knock, her door opened a crack. Amanda peeked in. "A woman is waiting to see you in the den."

Erica sighed. The last thing she needed was a visitor. "I'll be ready in two minutes." She dressed then headed to the den and stopped dead in her tracks. "Hello, Aletha."

Tommy's mother turned in her direction. "We need to talk. In private."

Erica's back stiffened. Aletha was the last person she wanted to see. Was there a way to avoid this meeting?

"Please." Aletha's eyes pleaded.

Erica breathed deeply. "All right." She opened the sliding-glass doors.

Seemingly evading eye contact, Aletha stepped out and settled on a chair.

Erica sat across the table from her. "What's on your mind?"

"The last time we met, I believed...no, I hoped...a traumatic experience would prove our children are too young to be in a serious relationship."

Erica's back stiffened. Somehow she had to defend the young couple without alienating Tommy's mother.

"Then today when my son came home from the hospital—" Aletha paused for a long moment. "I realized something I had failed to recognize or refused to see." She faced Erica. "It doesn't matter if they're young. Tommy loves your daughter from the depths of his soul." Her eyes reddened. "It's not easy admitting I was wrong, or accepting that Abby is the woman in his life now."

Relief mingled with compassion as Erica scooted her chair beside Aletha. "I imagine mothers of only children have a more difficult time letting go."

Tears spilled down Aletha's cheeks. "I'm proud of the man my son has become."

Erica placed her hand on the woman's arm. "You raised him well."

Aletha swiped her fingers across her cheeks. "I listened to Nancy's Nugget's podcast the day she interviewed you and your partners. You said it's important to pay attention when God puts people in your path who want to make your life better. At the time I refused to believe your comment applied to Tommy." She paused. "Which is why last May I discarded your invitation to Hilltop Inn's open house before my husband came home."

"I don't need to leave for another twenty minutes. If you have time, I can give you a private tour now."

"You don't mind?"

"Not at all." Erica stood and led the way to the gate leading from the backyard. "Did I mention that Abby is the vice president of our little company?"

"She's really smart, isn't she?"

"Yes, she is. Which is why she fell in love with your son."

Aletha smiled. "I believe you and I are destined to become good friends."

"So do I." Erica linked arm's with Tommy's mother as they crossed the driveway to the sidewalk fronting the inn. "Ten months ago, this old house was in serious need of repair. All the shrubs were dead. Peeling paint and mildew marred the façade." Erica pointed to the top of the turret. "Shingles were missing which caused the ceiling in the upstairs turret to cave in."

"I can't believe how much you accomplished in so short a time."

They stepped onto the porch. "Desperation and a lot of luck." Erica unlocked the front door and stepped inside. "Welcome to Hilltop Inn."

Aletha moved closer to the downstairs turret room. "Did you hire a decorator?"

Erica shook her head. "We couldn't afford a professional."

"You obviously didn't need a pro."

Following the tour, Erica escorted Tommy's mother to her car.

Aletha removed her keys from her purse. "If you don't mind, I want to visit Abby before I go home."

"Better yet. How about joining us for a picnic in her hospital room." Erica explained.

"Perfect. I'll meet you there."

A half-hour later, Erica carried four orders of burgers, fries, and shakes into the hospital lobby.

Aletha stood next to the entrance holding a colorful floral arrangement. "Lunch smells delicious."

"My stomach grumbled all the way over. Gorgeous flowers." Erica led the way to Abby's room. Inside, Tommy sat on the side of the bed holding Abby's hand. "Hey, kids, I brought a special visitor."

"Good timing. Abby came back from therapy five minutes ago." Tommy continued to hold her hand as he lifted off the bed.

Abby waved. "Hey, Mrs. Bennett."

Aletha set the flowers on the cabinet then stood across from her son. "How was therapy?"

"You mean my first torture session. My description is a lot more interesting than therapy, don't you think? Anyway, I worked up a ginormous appetite."

"Time to celebrate with a lunch for champions." After serving the items, Erica and Aletha sat on the bench while Tommy and Abby shared the tray table.

Abby swallowed a bite of burger. "Tomorrow I'll learn how to move out of a wheelchair by myself. By the time I go home, I'll be independent—except for driving—until my spinal cord heals enough for me to walk."

Erica sipped her milkshake. Had a medical professional predicted her outcome, or was the comment a product of Abby's own determination? Only time would tell.

Chapter 17

Tomato and cheese aromas wafted through the kitchen as Wendy grabbed her ringing phone off her granite counter and pressed Face-Time. "Hey, Kayla. What's up?"

"I'm studying for an algebra test—something I don't understand. I have a calculator on my phone, so why do I need to learn this math?"

"I asked the same question until I became Awesam's chief financial officer. Believe me, one day you'll need math skills."

"If I pass the test. How's my sweet little nephew doing?"

"Ryan's such a happy baby." Why hadn't her half-sister mentioned Cynthia? "What's going on with your brother and sister?"

"My brother's as pesky as ever. My sister not so much." Kayla looked away. "I don't understand why parents think they need to hide the truth from their kids."

Wendy headed to the French doors leading to the back deck. "Since I've become a parent, I understand how protecting our children is a natural instinct."

"I'm not a child, and no matter how hard Mom tries to put on a happy face, I can tell she's sick."

"Have you asked her?"

"More than once. Every time she told me there's nothing to worry about. If you ask me, she's in total denial."

A squirrel scampered across the deck railing. "Or she's telling you the truth."

Chris stepped beside Wendy and slid his arm around her shoulders. "Your brother-in-law wants to say hi." She held the phone in front of him.

He smiled. "Hi, Kayla."

"Let me ask you something." Kayla tilted her head. "You're a lawyer. Do you ever use algebra?"

"Not your favorite subject, right?"

Kayla rolled her eyes. "Hardly."

"To answer your question, even lawyers need algebra."

Kayla's eyes widened. "Are you serious?"

"Yeah, so keep studying. How's your mother?"

"Wendy will tell you. I've gotta go, we'll talk more later." Kayla ended the call.

Wendy spun away from the doors and set her phone on an end table beside a recliner. "Despite Cynthia's denials, Kayla still believes her mother is sick."

"Did she explain why?"

"Not this time." The doorbell sent Duke scampering across the open space. Wendy's brows pinched. "Are you expecting company?"

"Nope." Chris followed Duke and pulled the front door open.

Wendy stared wide-eyed at their visitors.

"We apologize for bothering you at home, but we need your help."

"Not a problem. Come on in." Chris stepped aside and motioned their visitors in. "Can I bring you a couple of beers?"

Brad Barkley stepped across the threshold. "Please." Jimmy followed on his crutches. "Make it two."

"Coming right up."

While Chris headed to the kitchen to grab their drinks, Wendy led their guests to the sofa. Chris returned, handed the beers to their guests, and took a seat on a recliner. Wendy propped her hip on the arm beside him. Chris tilted his beer toward Brad and his son. "What's going on?"

"An hour ago, I bailed Jimmy out of jail. Richard Watson had him arrested—"

Wendy gasped. "Who's Richard Watson?"

"Our district attorney." Chris leaned forward. "What's the charge?"

"Reckless endangerment."

Chris's eyes narrowed. "Are you serious?"

"It's a trumped-up charge."

"Obviously." Chris's jaw clenched. "What beef does Richard have with Jimmy?"

"With me, not Jimmy." Brad released a heavy sigh. "Two years ago, I expelled his son for selling drugs on campus. Despite Richard's claim his boy had been framed, the evidence against the kid was overwhelming. The suspension kicked him off the football team and cost him a scholarship to an elite university. Now his old man is out for revenge."

"This isn't the first time Richard has abused his position." Chris's tone failed to mask his disgust. "You'll need a good lawyer—"

Jimmy nodded. "Which is why we're here."

"Good. I'll take your case, and I'll win. Have either of you had dinner?"

Brad shook his head.

"Well then." Wendy lifted off the chair arm. "You'll eat with us."

"Jimmy and I don't want to disrupt your evening any more than we already have."

"Nonsense. Chris and I enjoy company. Besides, I have plenty of lasagna. So, what do you say?"

Brad glanced at his son. "Do you mind?"

He shrugged. "I guess not."

"All right, then." Eager to share the latest development with Erica, Wendy scooped her phone off the end table. She scurried to the kitchen and typed a message then pressed send.

Erica pulled her phone from her pocket. A pain erupted in the back of her throat as she read Wendy's text. "I'll be back in a minute." She headed out to the hall and smiled at a patient pushing his stand. After he passed by, she typed a response. "Are they worried?"

"My talented husband took the case. What do you think?"

Wendy obviously believed in Chris, and he had done an excellent job defending them against Gunter. Could he defeat a district attorney out for revenge? Erica stared at her phone.

"No one knows I'm texting you. We'll talk tomorrow."

Erica responded with a thumbs-up. A desire to comfort Brad overwhelmed her. Except if she called him tonight, he'd know Wendy had shared the news. She couldn't betray her partner's trust. Erica heaved a heavy sigh then pocketed her phone and returned to Abby's room.

Tommy and her daughter sat side by side on her bed playing a computer game on his iPad. Abby looked up. "Is everything okay, Mom?"

"Everything's fine, sweetheart." Erica moved to the window. Dusk had settled over Blue Ridge. How long before the news about Jimmy's arrest became public knowledge? Somehow she had to find the right moment to tell Abby and reach out to Brad—as a friend.

During dinner Wendy's heart ached for Jimmy. His silence and downcast eyes while his dad and his attorney discussed legal strategy made it clear he suffered from excruciating remorse. At some point Chris seemed to recognize the young man's agony and changed the subject to sports.

By the time she and Chris escorted their guests to the front door, the tension gripping Wendy's muscles had escalated to a headache. "I can't help but feel sorry for Jimmy. Granted he made a terrible mistake, but being subjected to the DA's wrath is beyond fair."

"One fact every attorney knows—life isn't fair."

"Have you tried a lot of cases against the DA?"

"A fair amount."

"Did you win?"

"Not all of them." Chris moved behind Wendy and massaged her shoulders. "You told Erica, didn't you?"

Wendy spun toward her husband. "How did you know?"

"I noticed you texting, and I know how close you and your partners are."

"I only told Erica the DA had Jimmy arrested, nothing more."

Chris stroked her cheek. "Brad and Jimmy opened the door when they decided to meet here instead of my office."

"I won't say a word to anyone else."

"It won't be long before the case becomes public knowledge." Chris strode to the kitchen and pulled a beer from the fridge. "Richard Watson has abused his position one too many times." He twisted off the cap and took a sip. "Someone needs to run against him next year."

Wendy joined him. "What about you? You're the best lawyer in town, and you're honest."

"Entering into politics is the last thing I want to do." Chris leaned back against the counter. "Besides if I ran and won, I'd take a cut in pay."

"What's more important? Money or integrity? Besides, my income as Awesam's CFO will continue to increase, and my shopaholic habit is almost totally cured."

Chris chuckled. "I appreciate your confidence, but I prefer defending clients over sending them to jail. However, if someone else decides to run, I'll help him or her raise a truckload of money to defeat DA Watson."

"So will I."

"No one would be able to resist your charm. About Jimmy's case—"

"I know. Everything you guys discussed about the case during dinner falls under attorney-client privilege." Wendy tilted her head. "Know what I think?"

"I need to help you clean up the kitchen?"

"Yeah, but also one day you should run for judge."

Chris laughed. "You're determined to plunge me into the political arena, aren't you?"

"I know how important the judge was in Gunter's murder trial."

"A future judgeship isn't entirely out of the question." Chris stroked her cheek. "If I ever decide to run—and that's one giant if—you'll be the first to know."

Chapter 18

Following a restless night, Erica opened her eyes and squinted at the early morning sun shining behind Tommy's head. After raising her recliner to a sitting position and plucking her phone off the end table, she moved to the bench beneath the window. "Why don't you go eat breakfast while Abby's still asleep?"

"Good idea." Tommy set his iPad aside. "What can I bring you?"

"Toast and coffee...unless there's a chicken biscuit."

"Done."

The moment Tommy walked out, Erica texted Wendy. "Are you awake?"

"I just fed Ryan."

"Okay to call you now?"

"Perfect time."

Erica tiptoed past Abby's bed into the hall and pressed Wendy's number.

Awesam's CFO answered before her phone rang. "How's our girl doing this morning?"

"She's still asleep." Erica moved toward the end of the hall. "What can you tell me about last night's dinner with Brad and Jimmy?"

"You understand anything I tell you has to stay between the two of us?"

"Of course."

"I can't say a word about the case, but I can share my impressions."

"Fair enough."

"Even though I don't know Brad well, I could tell he's furious about the trumped-up charges, and Jimmy's a wreck. Sorry for the choice of words. Anyway, he barely spoke the entire time they were here. It won't be easy for either one of them once the news goes public." Wendy paused. "Brad needs you now more than ever."

Erica's shoulders slumped. Did Wendy suspect the tension between her and Brad? Whether she did or didn't, her partner deserved to know the truth. "The last time we spoke...I was afraid the accident had damaged our relationship beyond repair."

"Because you were both still in shock?"

"After Abby forgave Jimmy, Brad told me he didn't want to lose me."

"How did you respond?"

Erica hesitated. "I told him I needed more time."

"Even though I'm fourteen years younger than you, do you mind if I give you a piece of advice?"

Erica moved her phone to her other ear. "You'll tell me whether I say yes or no, won't you?"

"Yeah, so here goes. Abby knows you're in love with Brad, right?"

"She does."

"When your daughter forgave Jimmy, she granted you permission to do the same. Beyond forgiveness, continuing your relationship with Brad will honor her and erase any blame she would experience if you broke up."

A stab of guilt pricked Erica's conscience. "You're a wise woman, Wendy."

"Eight months ago, I was miles away from having even a smidgen of wisdom. Then I married the smartest guy in town. So, what are you gonna do about Brad?"

"I don't know yet."

"Don't wait too long to make a decision, and it's okay if you tell him you know about Jimmy's arrest."

Dr. Kennedy rounded a corner and headed in her direction. "Abby's neurologist is on his way over."

"Call me as soon as you have an update."

"I will." Erica pocketed her phone then hastened back up the hall. "Good morning."

"How's our patient?"

"She was still asleep a few minutes ago." Erica followed him into the room.

Dr. Kennedy pulled the blanket away from Abby's leg then ran his fingernail along the top of her shin.

Her eyes fluttered open.

"You felt my touch, didn't you?"

"A little."

"Which is why I'm sending you home after today's therapy session. However, your work has just begun. I've scheduled therapy every day for the next seven days, then three times a week."

"For how long?"

"As long as it takes."

Tommy returned. "Hey, Doctor."

"How are you doing, young man?"

"A whole lot better since Abby's awake."

She raised her bed to a sitting position. "When can I return to work?"

"Well now, that depends."

Abby's eyes widened. "On what?"

"Your pain level."

"What if I tell you it's barely a three?"

"Is it?"

She shrugged. "Most of the time."

He chuckled. "You are one determined young woman."

"So, what's your answer?"

"You can return to work as soon as you feel ready."

"How about tomorrow?"

"Absolutely. Now for my pre-release instructions. From here on out, everyone needs to treat you the same as they would if you weren't in a wheelchair. The more you do on your own, the better your chance for a full recovery."

"Don't you worry about me, Dr. Kennedy. No matter how long it takes, I will walk again."

"I admire your spirit. I've scheduled a follow-up appointment in my office for two weeks from today. Until then, keep your positive attitude." Her doctor pulled the blanket back over her leg, then walked out.

An hour after Abby's therapy session ended, Erica walked beside Tommy as he wheeled her daughter out to his late-model sedan. Abby moved from the wheelchair onto his passenger seat without help. Erica touched her daughter's shoulder. "That was one impressive move,"

Abby grinned. "Yeah, I know."

After stashing her wheelchair in the trunk, Tommy slid onto the driver's seat. "Where to, Ms. Nelson?"

"Hmm. Before you take me home, I want to go see my car."

Erica leaned down. "Are you sure you're ready, sweetheart?"

Abby scoffed. "What was the last thing Dr. Kennedy told us, Mom?"

"I know."

"So, do you want to head home or go take a look at the damage?"

What I want to do is turn the clock back to the day of the wreck and tell you to stay at work an extra hour.

"What's your answer?"

Erica blinked. "I'll follow you." After dashing to the truck and placing her phone in the holder, she tapped Amanda's number. "We're pulling out of the parking lot now." She relayed Dr. Kennedy's instructions. "Which means we all need to treat Abby as if everything is normal. On the way home, she wants to check out the damage to her car."

"Our handyman finished installing the ramp at our front door a half-hour ago, so we're all ready for her to come home."

"Thanks for taking care of everything. I'll see you soon." Determined to remain calm, Erica focused on controlling her breathing while following Tommy. A sheriff's car passed going in the opposite direction. Was the driver the deputy who showed up at their front door the night of Abby's accident?

Tommy turned onto the wrecker-and-salvage company parking lot. Erica pulled up behind him. The moment she climbed out and rounded the front of the truck, her heart jumped to her throat. Her child's car was caved in from behind the driver's seat all the way to the taillight. The door window's glass was shattered. Erica eased beside Tommy's open passenger window.

Abby stared wide-eyed at the wreck. "If Jimmy had hit my car six inches closer to the front...do you know what that means?"

"You're lucky to be alive?"

"Yes, but also something else." Abby's lips curved into a smile. "I don't know what yet, but God protected me because He wants me to do something important."

Erica stared at the tangled metal. Her breath caught. Abby was right. Six inches had made the difference between life and death. Her child had summoned the courage to face an uncertain future with confidence.

"You can take me home now, Tommy."

Erica pressed her hand to her throat. Wendy, and now Abby, had shown wisdom far beyond their years. The time had come for her to do the same. She leaned down and peered into the car. "You two go on. I'll see you later."

"Where are you going?"

Erica smiled at her daughter. "To take care of something important."

"Insurance?"

"Sort of." Erica hastened to the truck and slid behind the steering wheel. Her muscles tightened as she backed away from Tommy's car. She braked at the road and glanced in her rearview mirror. Tommy had pulled up behind her. Gripping the steering wheel, Erica turned in the opposite direction from home.

Twice during the short drive, she fought the urge to change her mind. Seconds after parking at her destination and grabbing the door handle, doubt consumed her. Her limbs froze. Maybe she wasn't ready, after all. Except, if not now, when? Tomorrow? Next week? Digging deep for enough courage to follow through, Erica climbed out and headed straight to the building.

Inside, a receptionist looked up from behind a counter. "How can I help you?"

She hesitated. "I need to speak to the principal."

"Are you a parent?"

Erica swallowed the lump in her throat. "I am."

The woman lifted the handset and pressed a key. "A student's mother wants to speak to you." She listened. "All right." The woman set down the handset then nodded toward the right. "You can go on in."

Erica's heart pounded in her chest as she eased to the door. She breathed deeply to slow her pulse then knocked once, stepped inside, and closed the door behind her.

His eyes wide, Brad stood and moved in front of his desk. "How's Abby?"

Erica scanned his office. Pale blue walls. Gray metal desk. "Tommy's driving Abby home."

"What's the latest prognosis?"

"Dr. Kennedy is hopeful, and Abby's confident she'll walk again." She paused. "How's Jimmy holding up?"

"Abby forgiving him helped. He still has a long way to go before he forgives himself."

Erica eyed the artist's rendition of the high school on the wall behind Brad's desk. "Wendy told me about Jimmy's arrest. Chris is an excellent attorney."

"That's why I hired him to defend my son." Brad hiked his hip on the corner of his desk. "During the past few days, every time someone knocked on my door I hoped you'd walk in."

She broke eye contact and ambled to the window. "First Wendy, then Abby opened my eyes to the truth. Your son and my daughter have a lot of emotional and physical challenges to overcome. They don't need the added burden of guilt about us."

Brad followed and stood beside her. "Is their well-being the only reason you're here?"

"The first time I met Tommy's mother, she believed her son and Abby's love was too immature to survive a traumatic experience. This accident proved her wrong." Tears pooled and spilled down Erica's cheeks. "You and I need to discover if our relationship is strong enough to survive this valley we've been plunged into."

He brushed away her tears with a tenderness that reached in and touched her soul. "We'll take this journey one day at a time, my love." Brad wrapped his arms around her and pulled her close.

Erica's heart pounded in her chest. He had never called her 'my love' before. As much as she longed to tell him she loved him, the words refused to roll off her tongue. She pulled away. Her eyes met his. "Thank you for understanding."

He smiled. "Let me know when you're ready for another round of golf."

"I will."

Chapter 19

The moment Amanda pulled the dog bed across the hall to Abby's bedroom, Dusty lifted her head off her paws and thumped her tail on the floor in a lazy motion. "You know she's coming home today, don't you, girl?" Abby's canine companion responded with a muffled bark. "Yeah, you definitely know." Amanda leaned on the doorframe. If her own daughter, instead of Abby, was coming home in a wheelchair, could she find the courage to follow a doctor's orders and refrain from helping her with normal activities? She spun away and headed to the den, breathing in the mouthwatering scents of sugar and cinnamon. Dusty padded behind her and plopped on the floor beside the sliding-glass door.

Millie plodded in from the kitchen and set her cell phone on an end table. "All these years I've paid my premiums on time, and my insurance company can't move faster than a snail." Her tone screamed of frustration.

Amanda settled on a club chair. "What's the latest?"

"My agent claims they'll need another month before giving the construction crew the go-ahead. At this rate I won't have a home to return to until after Valentine's Day."

So much for hoping their houseguest would be in her own home by Christmas. Maybe this was God's way of stretching her patience. "We'll continue to make the best of our situation."

"Which is how I coped with Rupert all those years." Millie plopped onto the other club chair. "The man I married didn't have a romantic bone in his body, but he always gave me a dozen roses and a box of expensive chocolate on Valentine's Day."

"At least he tried."

"Was Preston romantic?"

Memories from her life with her soulmate triggered an involuntary smile.

"Your expression says yes." Millie crossed one leg over the other. "What's going on with Erica and Brad?"

"You need to ask Erica, not me."

"I don't want to pry—"

Amanda scoffed. "Since when?"

Millie pumped her foot. "There's a big difference between wanting to be involved and meddling. Especially since I'm an Awesam partner and I'm living in your house."

"Point taken. You still need to ask Erica."

"I will."

"Morgan called this morning. She's coming up this weekend."

Millie's head tilted. "Alone or with her husband?"

"Alone." *Because you're sleeping in our guest room, and every Hilltop room is booked.* "They'll both be here for Christmas."

"What about Thanksgiving?"

"They're flying to New Orleans to spend the holiday with Kevin's parents. This will be the first Thanksgiving I haven't spent with my daughter. At least Kevin's family plans to spend Christmas here. Including his grandmother, Miss Gertie. She reminds me of you."

"Because she's smart and talented?"

"More because she's feisty and says whatever's on her mind."

"Good for her. Odds are she also knows how to use a gun."

Amanda chuckled. "I wouldn't be surprised."

A car pulling up the driveway sent Dusty bolting to her paws and racing from the den.

Amanda scooted to the foyer and pulled the door open moments before Tommy wheeled Abby across the front sidewalk. "Welcome home."

Dusty planted her front paws on Abby's lap and greeted her with a face licking.

Abby's face scrunched. "I'm happy to see you too, girl." She eased Dusty off her lap.

"We all missed you." Millie pointed to Dusty. "Especially your sixty-pound lap dog."

Tommy pushed the wheelchair up the new ramp. "Something smells delicious."

"My special recipe and Abby's favorite cookie."

Abby's brows raised. "Snickerdoodles?"

Millie nodded. "I'm also making mac and cheese for your welcome-home party."

"With a big salad to keep you healthy," added Amanda. "Where's your mom?"

"Running an errand. Tommy's my official chauffeur. It's easy for me to maneuver from this chair to his car. Come on and I'll show you what I learned in therapy." Abby wheeled herself to the den. Tommy pulled a chair away from the table. Dusty padded behind them and sprawled on her belly under the table. Abby lowered the wheelchair arm. Her grimace while hoisting her body over the wheel and onto the chair made it clear she still struggled from pain.

Tommy sat beside her. "Pretty cool, huh?"

Millie snapped her fingers. "Talk about a maneuver deserving a reward." She scrambled to the kitchen then returned and set a plate of snickerdoodles and a glass of milk in front of Abby.

She took a bite. "As delicious as ever. I'm going back to work tomorrow."

Amanda resisted suggesting she wait a few days.

"Good for you." Millie settled across the table from Abby. "I'm eager to hear all about your therapy."

After swallowing another bite of her cookie and a sip of milk, Abby shared details.

"When Rupert had a knee replacement, I had to bribe him to go to therapy. He was a stubborn old coot."

"No one will have to bribe me. Especially if my new therapist is as cute as the guy in the hospital." Her tone hinted of humor. "Although he wasn't nearly as good-looking as Tommy."

"Good thing." Tommy winked. "Although, if you end up with a cute female therapist, I might have to go in with you."

Amanda smiled at their playful banter. "Morgan's coming up for the weekend."

"Cool." Abby tilted her head. "With Kevin?"

"Just her."

"She can sleep in my room." Abby moved her body back to the wheelchair. "Come on, Tommy." He followed her as she wheeled her chair through the den and into the hall.

Millie folded her arms on the table. "One of these days, our girl will stand up and walk right out of her wheelchair."

Erica parked in the carport beside Tommy's car then headed straight to the kitchen. She tossed the keys in the bowl and set her purse on the counter. "How's Abby doing?"

Millie turned away from the counter. "The way she moves in and out of her wheelchair is impressive."

Erica walked into the den and sat on the sofa beside Amanda. "Millie's impressed by Abby's maneuvers."

"For good reason." After setting her laptop on the coffee table, Amanda glanced over her shoulder then leaned close to Erica. "You talked to Brad, didn't you?"

"How did you know?"

"Lucky guess. Is everything okay between you two?"

"Better than yesterday, but not as good as a week ago. I still need more time."

"Understandable."

Erica peered over the back of the sofa as Tommy pushed Abby into the den and positioned her at the end of the coffee table. "Thank you for bringing her home."

"You're welcome." Tommy hiked his hip on the sofa arm. "One of these days, she'll be driving herself."

Abby brushed her hair behind her ear. "In a car *I* choose instead of the ride Gunter gave me for my sixteenth birthday." Her tone hinted of bitterness.

Millie sauntered in from the kitchen. "Hopefully your insurance company will settle faster than mine. Anyway, I'll have dinner on the table in five minutes."

"I'll help you." Amanda lifted off the sofa and followed Millie to the kitchen.

Erica made a mental note to contact her insurance agent first thing the next morning. "How are you feeling, sweetheart?"

"I'm still sore but glad to be home. Tommy's gonna drive me to work at nine tomorrow morning, then bring me back at five."

He nodded. "I'll work in between."

Erica's admiration for the young man had escalated tenfold during the past few days. "Abby's blessed to have you in her life."

"Thank you, but I'm the one who's blessed. After our first date, I didn't want to go out with any other girl." He paused. "My mother thought I was too young to be involved in a serious relationship."

Erica stared wide-eyed at Tommy. "Did she say something?"

"Not directly. Lots of little comments here and there."

Abby's face beamed. "Now Mrs. Bennett understands how much we love each other."

Erica stifled a grin. How long before Aletha invited Abby to call her by her first name?

"Okay, everyone." Millie set a casserole dish on the table. "Your welcome-home mac and cheese is ready."

During dinner, conversation centered around Abby's new job and the kind of car she wanted. After they finished eating, she and Tommy spent the following two hours in her room watching a movie while Erica attempted to focus on reading a book. When he left, Erica stepped into her daughter's room and closed the door. "How was the movie?"

Abby leaned back against her headboard. "You're about to tell me something important, aren't you?"

Erica sat beside her. "You know me well."

Abby thumped her arm. "You are my mom."

How should she begin? Erica pulled her knee onto the bed. "When tragedy strikes, some couples survive. Others fall apart."

"You're talking about you and Mr. Barkley, aren't you?"

"After I left you and Tommy, I drove to his office." Erica paused. "This accident is giving Brad and me the opportunity to discover if our relationship is strong enough to endure any challenges the future might bring."

"What if Jimmy hadn't hit my car?"

Erica plucked Abby's bear off the bed and stroked the pink ribbon tied around its neck. "The night you and I escaped to the women's shelter, I vowed never to subject either of us to a toxic relationship again. Then I married a con man who already had two wives."

"You couldn't possibly have known that Brian Parker was really Gunter Benson until he arranged for you, Amanda, and Wendy to meet at Blue Ridge Inn. Besides, unlike Gunter and my father, Mr. Barkley is a good man."

"I know. The truth is—" Erica set the bear aside and drew in a deep breath. "I would rather remain single for the rest of my life than continue another relationship destined to fail."

"How will you know if you and Mr. Barkley are soulmates?"

Erica pressed one hand to her chest and the other to her forehead. "If my heart and my mind come into agreement."

Chapter 20

Responding to the bell, Amanda opened the front door to greet Friday afternoon's last arriving guests. "Welcome to Hilltop Inn, Mr. and Mrs. Carter. I'm Amanda Smith, one of the inn's owners. My partners and I are delighted you chose to celebrate your twenty-fifth anniversary with us. Is this your first visit to Blue Ridge?"

The woman glanced sheepishly at her husband as he pulled two suitcases into the foyer. "We've always celebrated on a beach with our children. But now, our youngest is away at college. So, we're here instead."

"You selected the perfect location to relax and enjoy each other." While Amanda checked them in and shared details about the inn, the husband seemed distracted. "Breakfast is served from eight until ten in the dining room."

Mrs. Carter fingered her wedding ring. "I scheduled a massage for ten o'clock tomorrow morning."

"Erica Nelson is our massage therapist as well as one of Hilltop's three owners. You'll meet her at breakfast." Amanda led them up the front stairs and unlocked the Azalea Suite. "This room offers a lovely view of our English country garden and spa."

Mr. Carter hoisted the suitcases onto luggage stands while his wife moseyed to the window. "This is the first time we've stayed at an inn instead of a hotel."

"We want our guests to feel as if they're visitors in a friend's home." Amanda placed the key on the dresser. "Let us know if there's anything we can do to make your stay extra special." She stepped into the hall running the full length of the second story and closed the suite door. Unless the new arrivals settled whatever was going on between them tonight, tomorrow during breakfast, they'd surely trigger Millie's suspicion radar.

After returning to the first floor and closing the guest book, Amanda stepped out to the front porch. A cool breeze nipped her cheeks as she made her way to the ranch house. Inside the kitchen, Millie spread icing onto a red velvet cake. Amanda breathed in tomato and cheese scents. "Mac and cheese yesterday to celebrate Abby coming home and lasagna to welcome Morgan. You're spoiling us."

"Have you moved beyond tolerating me living in your house?"

"I'm getting there."

Erica walked in. "Whether Amanda admits it or not, she can't resist your cooking."

"At least I have culinary skills going for me." Millie dipped her spatula into the icing. "Did you notice anything odd about our new arrivals?"

Amanda shrugged. "I'm still trying to determine what you consider strange. As far as I'm concerned, all five couples are normal."

"Yeah, well, I'll form my own opinion tomorrow morning."

"I'm sure you will." An engine purred in the driveway. "Morgan's here." Amanda rushed outside seconds before her daughter's late model car pulled into the carport. She opened the driver's door. "You look wonderful, honey."

Morgan climbed out and embraced her. "So do you, Mom."

"When did you trade cars?"

Morgan released her and pushed the door closed. "Two days ago. Now the only vehicle remaining from our life with Gunter is his truck."

Erica stepped out. "Next year your mom and I will trade it in for two cars."

"If you ask me, the sooner we all erase every trace of the con man from our lives, the better." Morgan pulled her suitcase from the back seat, then released the handle and followed Amanda and Erica into the kitchen.

Millie greeted Morgan with a smile. "How was your drive from Atlanta?"

"Pleasant after I drove out of the city. Smells as if you're cooking up a storm."

Amanda chuckled at her daughter's unintended double meaning.

"I have to earn my keep around here." Millie placed the icing bowl in the sink. "Since Mittens, Whiskers, and I are staying in the guest room, you'll bunk with Abby."

"How's Dusty handling the cats?"

"Erica and your mother don't cotton to felines, so my kitties don't leave my room."

Amanda pressed her lips tight. No way she'd disagree and risk Millie releasing her cats.

Erica nudged Morgan. "Abby's looking forward to spending time with you."

"How's she coping with her injury?"

"Better than any of us expected, thanks in part to Tommy's devotion. He stayed with her the entire time she was in the hospital and now he's her chauffeur." Dusty pawed the sliding-glass doors. "Another family member is eager to greet you." Erica slid the door open.

Dusty padded over, her tail setting her backside in motion. Morgan patted her head. "Hey, girl. I'm happy to see you too." Dusty's ears perked seconds before she bounded to the foyer.

Erica laughed. "Our canine equivalent of a doorbell."

The front door swung open. Tommy pushed Abby's wheelchair up the ramp.

Morgan scooted to the foyer, bent down, and hugged Abby's neck. "I've missed you."

Abby's face beamed. "Oh my gosh. You're wearing the sweater I gave you for Christmas."

"It's one of my favorites." Morgan straightened and faced Tommy. "It's nice to see you again."

"Same here. I'll give you two time to catch up." Tommy bent down and kissed Abby's cheek. "I'll see you tomorrow afternoon." He stood upright then walked out.

Abby's focus shifted to Morgan. "I can't wait to hear everything about your life since you married Kevin."

Millie dashed in. "While you two chat, we'll enjoy my world-class lasagna and Caesar salad."

Amanda laughed. "Humility isn't one of our chef's best-known qualities."

Millie propped her hands on her hips. "Honey, at my age modesty is a waste of time and effort."

Morgan chuckled. "Good point."

"Millie spoils us with scrumlicious dinners. Come on and I'll show you one of the neat tricks I learned at therapy." Abby wheeled to the den and moved her body from her ride to a dining room chair.

Morgan applauded. "Wow. I'm impressed."

"By the time I learn how to walk again, I'll be strong enough to challenge guys to arm wrestling matches and win."

The women gathered around the table. Following Erica's blessing, Amanda served wine while Millie plated the lasagna. "Tomorrow the entire Awesam team will lunch at Wendy's."

"I can't wait to meet her baby."

"Speaking of babies—" Millie pointed her fork at Morgan. "When are you and Kevin planning to start a family?"

Amanda glared at Millie. "Why are you asking my daughter such a personal question?"

"Am I or am I not part of this strange little family?"

Morgan touched Amanda's arm. "I don't mind." She faced Millie. "Kevin and I have a seven-year plan. His parents are loaning us the money to buy a house. We plan to pay them back in two years."

Millie's eyes widened. "You two must earn big salaries."

"Engineers are paid well. After we pay off the debt, we'll live on Kevin's income for three years and save mine. Because—and this is just between us—we plan to save enough to invest in our own firm and spend two more years building the business. After that, we'll start working on a family."

Millie raised a brow. "How old are you?"

"Twenty-two."

"Which means you'll be nearly thirty before you start trying to get pregnant."

Morgan chuckled. "Twenty-nine isn't ancient, Millie. Besides, do you know how much it costs to raise a family today? Kevin and I want to be financially stable before we take that step."

Millie stabbed a piece of lettuce with her fork. "Eleanor's husband—Warren, not Gunter—owned a business. Which is how they could afford their fancy vacation home. Rupert and I worked retail, so our little house was all we could afford. I'm not complaining, mind you. We managed to raise our son and send him to a good college. Still, I wouldn't wait too long if I were you."

"Point taken." Morgan turned toward her honorary sister. "Are you still studying child psychology?"

Abby nodded. "In two more years, I'll earn an online degree." After Abby shared details about her studies and her new job, the conversation shifted to Awesam and the inn.

Following dessert, Amanda sensed Morgan and Abby wanted time alone. "Why don't you two settle in while the three of us help our chef with kitchen duty."

Morgan yawned. "It has been a long day."

"All right, then." Abby lifted onto her wheelchair then motioned for Morgan to follow her.

Abby maneuvered her ride into her room followed by Dusty and Morgan. She spun her chair around and pushed the door closed, then pointed to one of the twin beds. "That one's yours."

"Thanks."

"You have a cool new car."

Morgan lifted her suitcase onto the bed. "Even better, the last remnant of Gunter is now history."

"You were better off ditching it voluntarily than having it crushed. Are you still angry about him deceiving your mother?"

"If Mom hadn't devoted nine years of her life to the scumbag, she might have met a man as good as my father. Now I don't know if she'll ever trust another man."

"I didn't think Mom would either, until she met my high school principal." Abby lifted her body onto her bed. "Did your mother tell you who crashed into my car?"

"She did." Morgan sat cross-legged on the other bed. "You're putting on a happy face for everyone, aren't you?"

Abby stared wide-eyed at her roommate. "How did you know?"

"For an engineer, I'm good at reading body language."

"Mom has a new career she loves, and she's dating a good man who loves her."

"And you don't want her to worry about you, right?"

"Tommy's the only other person who knows the truth." Abby released a heavy sigh. "I've done a lot of research. Only a little more than half the patients with my injury fully recover, and for some of those, it takes years."

"You're not giving up, are you?"

Abby shook her head. "I'll continue doing everything within my power to heal. At the same time, I'm facing reality." Dusty bounded onto the bed and plopped her head on Abby's lap. She stroked her dog's back. "There's a fifty-fifty chance I'll never walk again." Tears pooled and tracked down her cheeks.

Morgan sat beside her. "Thank you for confiding in me."

Abby swiped her fingers across her cheeks. "I told Mom I survived the accident because God has something special for me to accomplish."

"Was that an idle comment to reassure her, or do you believe what you said?"

"Both."

"I believe the power of prayer combined with hard work produces miracles."

"The same thing Tommy said."

"There you go. Confirmation from two highly reliable sources."

Abby clutched Morgan's hand. "I'm glad we're honorary sisters."

"So am I."

Chapter 21

Cold morning air released a crop of goosebumps on Erica's arms as she and Amanda stepped out from under the carport and headed to the inn. "Our daughters were still awake when I turned in at ten. They have a lot more in common now than when they first met last December."

"True." Amanda pulled her sweater tight across her chest. "You have a ten o'clock appointment with one of our new arrivals. In my opinion, Mrs. Carter and her husband seemed unhappy for two people celebrating their anniversary."

They crossed the side yard. "Maybe they're hoping to breathe new life into their marriage."

"The same idea I had when I first checked into Blue Ridge Inn, until I discovered my so-called husband had two other wives." Amanda stepped onto the sidewalk fronting the inn. "Maybe you'll learn something about our guest during her massage."

"Uh-oh. Either Millie's suspicious nature has rubbed off on you, or you've taken on the role as the inn's psychologist."

"You and Wendy nixed my idea to create a luxury retreat where women can form friendships and heal." Amanda nudged Erica's arm. "That doesn't prevent me from noticing when a guest is troubled."

"Some people might think you're snooping."

Amanda followed Erica onto the front porch. "If you had plugged your ears when your massage client revealed personal information, you wouldn't have discovered Janice Williams had checked into our inn with your ex, or that he had abused her."

"Listening to a client is different." Erica unlocked the front door.

"How?"

"I don't know. It just is." Erica stepped into the foyer.

Amanda followed then pushed the door closed. She leaned close to Erica. "Just humor me and pay attention to Mrs. Carter."

"Only if she talks." Erica followed the scent of freshly brewed coffee to the kitchen.

Sabrina removed a bowl from the fridge. "Good morning."

Amanda eyed her. "Since none of our guests are checking out today, I'm surprised you're here."

"I figured Millie would need my help." Sabrina scooped yogurt into the fruit cups lined up on a tray. "Hilltop is such a fun place to work. I've been wondering—with only seven guest rooms, is this a money-making business?"

Erica stared at their housekeeper. Why did she want to know?

Amanda spun toward Sabrina. "If you're asking because you're worried about us paying you, relax."

Sabrina shrugged. "I'm not worried, just curious. When the train doesn't bring tourists from Blue Ridge to McCayesville, the restaurant where I work part-time barely scrapes by."

Millie tapped Sabrina's arm. "Go on and carry those fruit cups to the table."

"Yes, ma'am." She carried the tray into the dining room.

Millie turned her back to the door. "See what I mean about her asking all sorts of personal questions?" She spoke barely above a whisper. "Which I don't answer."

Erica poured a cup of coffee. "Maybe questions are her way of showing interest in her job."

"If you ask me, she's up to something."

Erica added sugar and creamer to her coffee. "In my opinion, you're overreacting."

"Yeah well, I plan to keep a close eye on her."

Sabrina returned to the kitchen. "A lady is already waiting in the living room."

Amanda motioned to Erica. She followed her partner to the pocket-door opening. "That's her." Amanda stepped into the living room. "Good morning, Mrs. Carter."

The woman spun away from the front window. "I hope I'm not too early."

"Not at all. Meet Erica Nelson, your massage therapist."

Erica approached her client with her hand extended. "It's a pleasure." The woman's limp handshake and sad eyes spoke volumes. Erica released her hand. "I understand you're celebrating your anniversary this week-end."

She nodded.

Amanda's head tilted. "Does Mr. Carter plan to join us for breakfast?"

She looked away. "He's on his way to play golf."

"You'll have plenty of company during breakfast, beginning with this lovely couple." Amanda smiled at the Dogwood Suite guests strolling into the living room. "Mr. and Mrs. Jones, meet Mrs. Carter."

The moment the new arrival approached, Amanda and Erica moved to the dining room. "You have to admit I'm right about Mrs. Carter being one unhappy woman."

"I see your point, but that doesn't change the fact that we're innkeepers who provide hospitality, not psychologists who solve guests' problems."

"All I'm asking you to do is pay attention during her massage."

"To what end?"

"After all the marital trauma we've experienced, we're well qualified to share a few words of wisdom."

"Only if she asks." Erica returned to the kitchen. During the following two hours, every attempt to shrug off Amanda's comments failed. Questions swirled through her mind. Hadn't Abby chosen to use her experience to help children from troubled homes? Why shouldn't Gunter's wives club members help other women? Where was the line between hosting guests and becoming involved in their personal lives? By the time her client arrived for her appointment, confusion had reduced Erica's brain to mush. She forced a smile. "Did you enjoy breakfast?"

Mrs. Carter nodded.

"Is this your first massage?"

Avoiding eye contact, she glanced around the room. "In a long time."

Summoning her warmest smile, Erica explained what to expect. "Let me know when you're ready." She left her client alone while debating whether to wait for her to speak or ask questions. Five minutes after stepping into her office, Mrs. Carter hadn't responded. Erica opened the door a crack. "I didn't hear you if you called me."

"I forgot."

Erica peeked in. Her client lay face down on the massage table. "You want a deep-tissue massage, right?"

"I think so."

"Let me know if the pressure is too much." One stroke along Mrs. Carter's knotted shoulder muscle relayed everything Erica needed to know about the woman she had yet to see smile. Maybe it was time to ignore her rule to remain quiet unless her client engaged in conversation. "Have you visited Blue Ridge before?"

"This is our first time."

"You chose the perfect place to celebrate your anniversary. Is it today or tomorrow?"

"Today."

"How fun. Where are you having dinner?"

"We didn't make reservations."

"I can recommend a few places."

No response.

Her client obviously wasn't in the mood to chat. Erica remained silent during the remainder of the hour-long massage. When finished, she stepped into her office to allow Mrs. Carter time to dress.

"Ms. Nelson?"

Erica stepped back into the massage room. "Yes?"

Her client handed her a generous tip.

"Thank you."

"I've been wondering." She paused. "Are you married?"

"Divorced."

Mrs. Carter glanced at Erica. "Would you...I mean do you have time to talk?"

Maybe attempting to chat hadn't been a waste of time after all. "I do, and now is the perfect time to enjoy our garden." Erica pocketed her phone then escorted her client from the spa to the stone path leading to the gazebo. "You're welcome to call me Erica."

"I'm Julie." They made their way to a bench facing the three-tier fountain. "About your divorce...did your husband leave you?"

The woman sitting beside her needed a confidante, so why not tell her the truth? "I left him because he couldn't control his fists."

"While my husband and I were dating and during our first year of marriage, we were so much in love and totally devoted to each other. When our first child was born, I quit my job to become a stay-at-home mom." Julie fingered her wedding rings. "During the following years, I devoted all my energy to raising our two girls while my husband immersed himself in his career and golf."

Julie moved to the fountain and sat at the pool's edge. "When our second child left for college I realized how little my husband and I had in common. Even when he's home, we barely talk to each other. He's a decent man, so I don't believe he's cheating on me. Maybe if I had spent more time on my marriage—" Her voice faltered. "Tom fell out of love with me a long time ago."

Erica sat beside Julie and twirled her fingers in the water. "Maybe it's time to help him fall in love with you again."

Julie sighed. "After all these years, I don't know how."

Their guest had reached out to her, so why not try to help? "I have an idea. Wait here." Erica stepped away then pulled her phone from her pocket and pressed Amanda's number.

"How'd the massage go?"

"Better than I expected. I have an idea." She explained. "What do you think?"

"You finally understand why I pushed for my original idea."

"All right then." Erica pocketed her phone and returned to the fountain. "I'm inviting you to join me and my partners for lunch."

"Are you sure no one will mind me tagging along?"

"Our chief executive officer is thrilled. Plus, you'll meet three beautiful young women who know all about falling in love."

Two hours after walking into Wendy's home, the Awesam team and Julie had agreed on a save-the-Carter-marriage strategy. Following lunch, Morgan, Abby, and Julie headed downtown to shop, while Amanda, Erica, and Millie returned to the inn and spent the remainder of the afternoon fleshing out the details.

Soft background music played in Hilltop's dining room as dusk settled over Blue Ridge. Amanda set the small table for two in front of the window. "If we could go back eight months, would you go along with my idea to create an escape for women?"

"Uh-uh." Erica lit two candles nestled in Eleanor's crystal holders. "Because today proves all we need is female intuition and an inquisitive chief information officer to respond to our guests' needs."

"Today also proves my idea has merit."

Millie swung the kitchen door open.

Amanda breathed in the rich lemon and butter scents. "Dinner smells delicious."

"Veal piccata, mashed potatoes, and Italian salad." Their chef placed a bottle of white wine in the chiller beside the table. "According to Julie, her husband's favorite meal."

"Phase one of our plan." Erica dimmed the chandelier over the long dining room table. "Phase two, create a romantic atmosphere. Phase three—" Her eyes widened. "Wow, you look amazing."

Julie sashayed into the dining room wearing a sexy red dress. "Your daughters applied my makeup. I hope it's not too much?"

"Anyone who walks by will swear you're a newlywed and not a woman celebrating twenty-five years. Has your husband seen you?"

Julie shook her head. "I texted him to meet me here at six-thirty."

Amanda glanced at her watch. "Which is three minutes from now. Time for phase three."

Erica and Millie scooted to the kitchen, leaving the door ajar. Julie stood beside the table for two. Amanda uncorked the wine and poured two glasses, then moved to the double-pocket doors.

Julie's husband descended the stairs then strode across the living room.

Amanda summoned her warmest smile. "Good evening, Mr. Carter."

His brow pinched. "What's going on?"

"A beautiful woman is waiting for you." Amanda motioned for him to enter.

Tom Carter stepped in. His jaw dropped. "Julie?"

"Happy anniversary, sweetheart."

Amanda closed the pocket doors. "Dinner will be served shortly." She strode to the kitchen, closing the door behind her. "A few weeks ago, our Awesam team prevented a disastrous marriage. Tonight, I believe we'll save one."

Chapter 22

Despite the Awesam partners speculating until midnight whether their save-a-marriage plan would make a difference, Erica awoke twenty minutes before her alarm. She crossed the hall to the bathroom, turned on the shower, and stepped into the tub. How many future opportunities would arise to go above and beyond for their guests?

After drying her hair and dressing, Erica headed to the den.

Amanda sat at the dining room table tapping her laptop keyboard. "Good morning."

Erica yawned. "How long have you been awake?"

"About an hour."

"You're obviously as eager as I am to find out what happened after we left the Carters last night."

"The thought crossed my mind." Amanda pushed her laptop aside. "Are you ready to head over?"

"More than ready." Erica hurried to the kitchen and grabbed keys off the counter. A cold gust nipped her cheeks as they stepped out to the carport and rushed across the side yard. She pointed to Hilltop's second story. "The light's on in the Azalea Suite, which means our anniversary couple is awake." They scurried along the sidewalk fronting the inn and stepped onto the porch. Erica unlocked the door and stepped into the foyer. Two of their guests scheduled to leave today carried coffee cups from the dining room to the living room. "Good morning."

Amanda followed Erica. "I hope you've enjoyed your stay."

The woman smiled. "Hilltop is right up there with Blue Ridge Inn as one of our all-time favorites. In fact, I posted a five-star review a few minutes ago."

Erica brushed hair away from her cheek. "My partners and I are delighted."

Amanda pressed her palms together. "Thank you for taking the time to post the review."

"My husband and I own a small business, so we understand the impact of reviews, and yours is well deserved."

After greeting a guest descending the stairs, they headed to the den. Erica leaned close to Amanda. "A favorable comparison to Blue Ridge Inn is a big deal."

"We couldn't ask for a better accolade." Amanda followed Erica into the kitchen. "What's for breakfast?"

Millie spun away from the sink. "Quiche and cheese grits. I've been thinking about last night, and in my opinion, we need to add a private dinner to Hilltop's options, prepared by award-winning Chef Millie, of course."

Erica chuckled. "What award?"

"The one the board's going to give me."

"Hmm." Amanda tapped her finger to her chin. "Your idea is interesting."

"The award or the private dinners?"

"Both."

Millie stared at Amanda. "Are you agreeing or humoring me?"

"Neither. However, we'll discuss your proposal at our next board meeting."

"If you go along with my idea, whatever you charge should include compensation for the chef."

Erica laid plates on the island. "We wouldn't expect you to work extra hours without paying you."

"Which makes you part of our overhead, Millie." Amanda chuckled. "Right up there with utilities and cleaning supplies."

Millie huffed. "You buy supplies at Walmart. Try hiring a chef as talented as I am for the little bit of salary you pay me."

Erica trilled her lips as she stepped between Awesam's president and chief information officer. "We couldn't manage without you. Right, Amanda?"

"Absolutely."

Millie huffed. "You don't need to boost my ego. I know I'm worth far more than you pay me, and don't forget you promised to give me a raise in January."

"Wendy has already worked our new salaries into next year's budget, which includes raises for everyone." Erica removed Hilltop's phone from her pocket. "A text from Sabrina. She's on her way."

Millie's mouth drew downward. "You're not giving her a raise, are you?"

Erica shook her head. "She's too new."

"Know what, Millie?" Amanda poured a cup of coffee. "You need to ditch the attitude about our housekeeper."

"I will when and only if she goes more than two days without prying into our business."

The door leading to the dining room inched open. "Do you have a minute?"

Grateful for the disruption, Erica pulled the door open. "Please join us. We're all eager to hear about last night."

Seemingly avoiding eye contact, Julie stepped in. "When I decided to spend our anniversary in this town instead of the beach, I had hoped a change of scenery would be the first step toward revitalizing our marriage." She paused and ran her finger along the island's smooth granite.

Erica exchanged a glance with Amanda then probed Julie's bland expression. Had their marriage been too far gone to save?

"Then last night Tom walked into the dining room and saw me wearing a sexy dress—I can't remember when I last saw that gleam in my husband's eyes. We talked more intimately during dinner than we have in a long time. After we finished Millie's delicious dessert, we held hands and strolled through the garden to the gazebo." A dreamy-eyed expression lit Julie's face. "Last night was the most romantic Tom and I have experienced since we were newlyweds."

Erica pressed her palms together then touched her fingertips to her lips. "We couldn't be more thrilled for you."

"Thank you all from the bottom of my heart for helping me transition from an empty-nest mother who misses her children to a desirable woman whose husband is falling in love with her all over again."

Millie grinned. "The Awesam team goes above and beyond to make our guests' stay extraordinary."

"Indeed, you do, and the private dinner was a stroke of genius."

Millie shot Amanda her best I-told-you-so look.

"Tom and I have already reserved the Azalea Suite for next year's anniversary."

Sabrina bounced in from the den. "Sorry I'm late."

"Anyway, thank you again, and please tell Morgan and Abby how much I appreciate their help." Julie pivoted and returned to the dining room."

Sabrina's head tilted. "What'd I miss?"

Erica smiled at the young woman. "Another Hilltop Inn success story."

"I've been wondering—"

"You wonder more than anyone I know." Millie grabbed an oven mitt.

"So, I'm curious. Big deal." Sabrina removed fruit cups from the cabinet. "Anyway, why did you ladies turn this house into an inn instead of selling it for a big profit?"

"Because Erica, Wendy, and Amanda are three of the smartest women you'll ever meet." Millie removed three quiche pans from the oven. "Enough with the chitchat. You need to fill those fruit cups and take them to the dining room."

"I'm on it."

Erica eyed Amanda's pinched expression. Was Awesam's president confused by their chef's comment, or did she regret suggesting she stop complaining about Sabrina? Whichever applied, at least Millie had refocused her assistant on the task at hand.

After serving the guests and observing Tom and Julie's upbeat demeanor, Erica and Amanda each carried a plate out the front door and across the yard. Inside the ranch house, Erica grabbed two forks on her way to the dining room table. "We brought you breakfast."

Morgan gripped her coffee mug. "Perfect timing."

Abby peered up at Erica. "We're dying to find out what happened with the anniversary couple."

Erica set the plate on the table then relayed Julie's comments.

Abby high-fived Morgan. "The sexy dress we talked Julie into buying did the trick."

Amanda sat beside her daughter. "Based on last night's success, Millie wants to offer private dinners to our guests. Since you're Awesam's official consultant, what's your opinion about her suggestion?"

166

"Hmm. A romantic dinner for two would appeal to some guests, and if we charge enough, it may favorably impact Hilltop's bottom line."

"Well then, we'll discuss the option during our next board meeting."

After enjoying each other's company for another hour, Morgan pushed away from the table. "This has been such a fun weekend, but I have a wonderful husband waiting for me to come home."

Abby hoisted herself into her wheelchair and followed Morgan down the hall.

Amanda yawned. "During the past hour, we've talked about everyone's romances except yours...and mine which doesn't exist."

"What's your point?"

"Have you accepted Brad's invitation to play golf next Saturday?"

Erica shook her head. "We haven't played since the accident, and never on Saturday."

Amanda raised an eyebrow. "Maybe playing golf on a different day is his way of coping."

"I don't know if I'm ready to spend four hours alone with him."

"If you ask me, he invited you because he wants to share more of his world with the woman he loves."

"I have one huge problem." Erica breathed deeply, then slowly released the air. "My heart and my mind are battling over a decision."

"Which one is preventing you from accepting his invitation?"

Erica tapped her forehead with one hand and her chest with the other. "Yesterday my brain. Today my heart."

Amanda patted Erica's hand. "Accepting his invitation could help synchronize your heart and mind."

Erica shrugged. "Or add to the confusion."

"There's only one way to find out."

Erica stared at her partner for a long moment, then pulled her hand away and rose.

"You're going to call Brad, aren't you?"

"If my courage doesn't disappear in the next thirty seconds."

Chapter 23

Wendy tiptoed away from the crib then stepped across the hall to their home office. She eased behind her husband hunched over his desk and massaged his shoulders. "Are you this tense every time you prepare to defend a client?"

"More so this time." He straightened his back. "Jimmy's trial is personal."

Wendy released his shoulders then pulled her desk chair beside him. "Because his dad is dating Erica, and she's family?"

"In part. When Brad was my football coach, every player loved him. We won nearly every game because he demanded our best. He inspired us to play as a team while challenging each of us to stretch beyond our perceived limitations." Chris brushed his fingers through his thick hair. "Coach Barkley did more to build character than any coach I ever had. If a kid broke the rules, he didn't hesitate to exact fair punishment, which didn't always go over well with parents."

"Including the DA?"

"Especially him. Reckless endangerment is a difficult case for the prosecution to prove and the defense to argue."

"You'll win, right?"

"I'll do everything legally possible to prove Jimmy's innocence." Chris nodded toward the window. "Mom's here."

Their black Lab's ears perked seconds before scrambling from the office.

"I'll see you later." Wendy kissed Chris's cheek then hastened to open the front door. "Thank you for coming over." She embraced her mother-in-law.

"It's easier for me to babysit here."

"Ryan's morning nap should end shortly." Wendy released Linda. "Oh, and Chris is working at home today."

"My grandson and I won't bother him." She patted Duke's head. "I'll keep this big lovable dog company."

"Don't let him sneak on the sofa." Wendy plucked her purse and laptop off the kitchen counter. "I shouldn't be gone more than a couple of hours."

"Take all the time you need."

Wendy scooted to the garage and climbed into her SUV. Ten minutes after pulling out of the driveway, she parked behind a sedan and hastened through the ranch house kitchen to the den. "Is the car parked beside the truck Abby's new ride?"

Erica shook her head. "It's a rental until our insurance company settles. Abby can maneuver in and out of the passenger seat on her own."

Wendy placed her laptop on the table, then sat between Erica and Amanda and across from Millie. "How's her therapy going?"

"Slower than I'd hoped."

Millie touched Erica's arm. "An injured spinal cord takes time to heal."

"I know, but waiting without knowing the outcome isn't easy."

"Which is another good reason to keep you busy." Amanda twisted the cap off a water bottle and took a sip. "As Awesam's president, I'm calling this board meeting to order."

"Starting with a discussion about my proposal." Millie slapped a sheet of paper on the table. "I've created five gourmet meals for our private dinners."

Wendy's brows pinched. "What dinners?"

"Those we're offering to our guests."

Amanda faced their chef. "Hold on to your chickens, Millie. We haven't decided one way or the other."

Wendy crossed her arms on the table. "Will someone please explain what you're talking about?"

Amanda pointed to Erica. "Go ahead, Ms. CEO."

"Based on the romantic evening we planned for Julie and her husband, Millie believes we should offer the same service to other guests."

"I see." Wendy eyed Awesam's president. "Did you run the idea by Morgan?"

Amanda nodded. "She believes the concept is worth considering, if we can figure out how to make it profitable."

Millie pushed the menu options to Wendy. "I already estimated food costs."

Wendy plucked the paper off the table then ran her finger down the list. She stopped at the last note. "Prepared by Award-winning Chef Mildred Cunningham?" Wendy eyed their CIO. "What award are you referring to?"

"The one you three will give me."

Erica chuckled. "One fact is undeniable. Our chef isn't too humble to toot her own horn."

Amanda swallowed another sip of water. "Now that we've confirmed Millie's penchant for self-promotion, we need our CFO to run the numbers."

Millie snapped her fingers. "Don't forget to add compensation for the chef."

Wendy opened a spreadsheet and entered expenses, chef compensation, and profit margin. After double-checking the results, she turned her laptop around. "Assuming Millie would also serve the meal, here's what we should charge."

Millie leaned close. "I obviously came up with a great idea."

Erica eyed the screen. "I agree."

"All right then, let's vote. All in favor of adding a private dining experience to our options, raise your hands. Millie's hand shot up first, followed by Erica and Wendy's. Amanda slapped her palm on the table. "Done. Given you're our chief executive officer in charge of team building, Erica, you have the privilege of creating an award for our infamous chef."

Millie huffed. "You meant to say famous, right?"

Amanda grinned. "Of course."

"Now onto more fun subjects." Erica tapped her keyboard. "Millie and Abby will manage Hilltop while the three of us spend the first weekend in December at Blue Ridge Inn."

Wendy pushed her laptop aside. "In the same rooms Gunter reserved for our first visit?"

Erica shook her head. "I reserved the lodge, which was Mountain Mama's Coffee shop before the owner relocated. The inn's owner transformed the space into a multi-guest suite."

"Ironic." Amanda leaned back. "Our exclusive wives club will celebrate our post-Gunter lives in the same space where Chris first told us the con man had willed the Harrington properties to the three of us."

"We can also spend time in the inn's parlor. For now, on to our next topic." Wendy tapped her keyboard. The partners discussed budgets and marketing plans until the doorbell rang.

"Perfect time for a break." Amanda pushed away from the table and headed to the foyer. Moments later she escorted Chris into the den. "Our attorney needs to talk to us."

Wendy's eyes widened. "About Jimmy's case?"

"No." Chris pulled a chair beside Wendy. "A half hour ago, I received a certified letter from Gunter."

Amanda dropped onto her chair. "What's the bum up to now?"

Chris's jaw tensed as he pulled a folded sheet of paper from his jacket pocket. "You'll understand why I'm bringing this to your attention." He unfolded the letter. "*Dear Wendy. When I accepted Chris Armstrong's bribe—*"

Wendy tapped Chris's arm. "What bribe?"

He hesitated. "Two grand added to his prison account in exchange for his release to all legal rights to his unborn child."

Amanda raised a brow. "Does he want more money?"

"Let me finish reading." Chris's focus returned to the letter. "*When I accepted Chris Armstrong's bribe, he failed to inform me about his personal relationship with you. After I learned he married you and adopted my son, I hired my own attorney to rectify two wrongs. First, to prove your husband requested the relinquishment of my legal rights under false pretenses—*"

Wendy gasped. "Can he win?"

"His claim is impossible to prove. Hold on, there's more. '*Second, to prove I was coerced into relinquishing the rights to my inheritance and therefore am entitled to reclaim Hilltop Inn and all future profits as my legal property.*'" Chris looked up. "This letter is from Gunter—which makes his claim about hiring an attorney highly suspect. However, even if he has retained counsel, rest assured he doesn't have a legal leg to stand on."

Chris folded the sheet of paper. "In addition to the letter, Gunter sent a two-page list of items he claims as his because they belonged to Eleanor Harrington. That list combined with all the other details proves someone is feeding him information."

Millie slammed her fist on the table. "All those questions Sabrina asked proves she's the culprit." She bolted to her feet. "I'm going next door and drag her butt over here—"

Chris aimed his palm at Millie. "Not a good idea."

She hesitated, then dropped back down. "You're not suggesting we let her off the hook, are you?"

"We need to use common sense. Which one of you supervises Sabrina?"

Erica lifted her hand. "Officially, I do."

"Call Sabrina and give her a logical reason to meet you here."

"Now?"

"Yes."

"All right." Erica grabbed her phone, then pressed their housekeeper's number and activated the speaker.

Sabrina answered after the second ring. "Hey. I just finished cleaning the last suite."

"Why don't you come over to the ranch house so I can show you Hilltop's office and give you an update on next week's schedule."

"I'll be on my way as soon as I put my supplies away."

"Good. I'll see you in a few." Erica ended the call.

"Well done. When she arrives, I need you ladies to resist saying anything and let me act as Awesam's attorney." Chris positioned a chair directly across from his seat. "Bring in a couple more bottles of water."

Amanda hastened to the kitchen and returned with three bottles.

Chris remained standing.

Silence hung heavy until the doorbell rang. Chris nodded toward Erica. "Go ahead."

She breathed deeply then released the air and headed to the foyer. "Come on in." She led Sabrina into the den.

Chris smiled. "Hello, I'm Wendy's husband." He extended his hand.

She accepted it. "I'm Sabrina."

"I hear you're doing a great job as Hilltop's housekeeper."

"It's a fun job."

He released her hand then motioned to the empty chair. "We're finishing up a board meeting, so please join us."

"Okay?"

Chris returned to his chair. "I'm also Awesam's attorney." Still smiling, he crossed his arms on the table. "How long have you known Gunter Benson?"

Sabrina's mouth fell open. "I...um...who?"

"Are you aware he's serving time for murder and that he cons women into believing he's innocent?" Chris's tone remained calm, almost reassuring.

Hilltop's housekeeper fidgeted. "I don't know what you mean."

"Mr. Benson has come into information that could only come from someone who's familiar with Hilltop Inn and is in close contact with my clients."

The color drained from Sabrina's face.

Chris's eyes remained trained on the young woman. "Although you've made a foolish decision, technically you haven't broken the law. At least not yet."

Sabrina's eyes bulged. "What do you mean by 'not yet'?"

"Lying when confronted by indisputable evidence *is* unlawful."

"I...don't actually know him."

"Are you saying you've never met Gunter Benson face-to-face?"

Sabrina nodded.

"However, you have communicated with him, right?"

After a long moment, she nodded again.

"Now that we've established a relationship, tell us how he first contacted you."

Sabrina's eyes darted from Chris to Wendy, then back to Chris. "He sort of sent me a letter."

"I see. Have you ever been to Las Vegas?"

"No."

"Then help me understand. You've never met Gunter Benson personally, yet he knew your name and address?" Chris tapped his fingers on his forearms. "How is that possible?"

"Um..." Sabrina wrapped a lock of blue hair around her finger. "My boyfriend...well, he's in the same prison. I guess he told Gunter about me."

"That makes sense. You're a smart young woman, so how did a convicted felon convince you to spy on my clients?"

"Gunter promised to pay me and my boyfriend a lot of money to help him reclaim what rightfully belonged to him. If I'd known he killed someone..." Her voice quivered. "Am I in trouble?"

"That depends on whether or not you continue to tell the truth."

"I promise I won't lie."

"Good. Tell us everything you told him about Hilltop Inn and my clients."

Following her confession, Sabrina's bottom lip quivered. "Is there any chance you'll let me keep my job?"

"Not one chance in a million!" Millie's comment erupted as if she could no longer control her emotions.

"I'm sorry, Sabrina." Erica folded her hands on the table. "Given the circumstances, we don't have any other choice but to let you go." She held out her hand. "You need to return the inn's key."

Their housekeeper fished the key from her pocket and placed it in Erica's hand. "I'm sorry I trusted a prisoner over you ladies."

"So are we."

"Before you leave—" Chris removed another paper and a pen from his jacket pocket and pushed it across the table. "You need to sign this document."

"What is it?"

"An agreement to cease all communication with Gunter Benson and refrain from sharing any information about Hilltop Inn or my clients with anyone else. Or you will be prosecuted for fraud."

Sabrina's eyes reddened as she reached for the pen. Seconds after signing, she rose then scurried to the foyer and out the front door.

Wendy tucked her hair behind her ear. "I sort of feel sorry for her, especially since she's one more innocent victim of a smooth-talking con artist."

Millie scoffed. "Sabrina sold us out for money. I don't feel one bit sorry for her."

Amanda nudged their chef's arm. "Know what? For once you and I agree."

Chapter 24

Three days after firing Sabrina, Erica gripped the front doorknob. How could she avoid making another huge hiring mistake? Let Amanda make the decision. Except staff was her responsibility. The bell rang a third time. She drew in a deep breath and slowly released the air, then pulled the door open. "Ms. Wagner?"

The middle-aged woman with dark hair sprinkled with gray and twinkling brown eyes smiled. "Everyone calls me Bernie, short for Bernice."

"I'm Erica Nelson. Please come in." She escorted the candidate to their living room turned office and pointed to a chair.

The woman sat and laced her fingers on her lap. "Thank you for taking the time to interview me."

"You're welcome." Erica glanced at Chris's background check. Nothing suspicious about this candidate. But then there was nothing dubious about Sabrina's information either. She turned the paper face down and turned her chair toward Bernie. "Why don't we begin by you telling me a little about yourself."

"Well, I'm sixty-one years old." She paused. "Oh dear, I don't believe I'm supposed to tell you my age, am I?"

When did she last apply for a job? "I can't ask, but there's nothing wrong with you volunteering the information. What else can you tell me?"

"My husband passed away six months ago from a massive heart attack."

"I'm so sorry."

"It was his third so not unexpected. Anyway, I've spent the last thirty-two years raising three children. Not one of them moved back to Blue Ridge after graduating from college. Now I live alone with nothing to keep me busy. Even though I haven't held a paid job in more than a quarter century, I'm reliable, and when it comes to cleaning, I'm an expert."

"Taking care of a family and a home is important work."

"My friend Faith, who's also Blue Ridge Inn's assistant innkeeper, suggested I apply for the job."

"I met Faith last December when I checked into the inn. How long have you two been friends?"

"Since long before she took the job at Blue Ridge Inn. We go to the same church. Anyway, I live three minutes away from here, so I'm practically a neighbor."

Given that no one other than Bernie had applied, and Faith seemed a good judge of character, Erica described the housekeeping duties and the pay.

"I'm willing to do whatever you need, Ms. Nelson. Not because I need the money, which I don't." Bernie scooted to the edge of her chair. "Faith loves her job, especially meeting new people. Even though I don't have professional experience, serving breakfast with a smile every morning and preparing rooms for a lovely visit would satisfy your guests' desires for a wonderful vacation and my need to do something meaningful."

Impressed by the woman's honesty and pleasant demeanor, Erica stood. Time for the most important test before making an executive decision. She touted their chef's expertise while escorting her applicant from Awesam's office to Hilltop's kitchen. "Millie, meet Bernie, our housekeeper applicant. She and Faith are good friends."

Hilltop's chef wiped her hands with a towel. "Finally, a normal candidate."

"I'm as normal as they come." Bernie's face lit with a smile. "I hear Hilltop's guests rave about your gourmet breakfasts."

Millie's chest puffed. "And my private dinners, although I've only served one thus far."

"Do you use recipes or natural talent?"

"A little of both." After chatting for five more minutes, Millie spun toward Erica. "Have you given Bernie the tour?"

"I wanted to introduce you two first."

"I see. Excuse us for a moment, Bernie." Millie motioned for Erica to follow her to the dining room. "You want to find out if I approve before offering her the job, don't you?"

Erica stared at her. "The final decision is mine; however, your opinion counts."

Millie folded her arms across her chest. "Because I was right about Sabrina?"

"Good working relationships are important to creating exceptional guest experiences."

"That's a bunch of CEO gobbledygook. You want to know if she passes the Millie test."

No point wasting time denying the truth. "Well, does she?"

"Definitely." Millie spun around and headed back to the kitchen. "Awesam's chief executive officer is ready to show you the inn now."

Resisting an eye roll, Erica ambled to Bernie. "We'll begin in the dining room while our chef finishes up in here." Following a tour of the first floor and the second-story hall and supply closet, Erica escorted her candidate to the inn's backyard.

Bernie stooped and fingered the sign dedicating the garden to Eleanor. "Millie reminds me of my eighty-year-old aunt—crusty on the outside but soft inside." She straightened. "If you introduced us to find out if I can get along with her, the answer is yes."

Erica chuckled. "I believe our chef has met her match. Are you available to begin your new role as Hilltop's housekeeper tomorrow morning?"

"Yes, I am."

"Although breakfast is normally from eight to ten, Sunday we serve an hour earlier so we can all attend eleven o'clock church services. That means we'll need you at six-thirty."

"I'll be here, and thank you for giving me this opportunity."

Pleased with her decision, Erica squared her shoulders and escorted their new housekeeper across Hilltop's parking pad.

Seconds after they stepped onto the side yard, Amanda drove the truck up the ranch house driveway and parked in the carport. She stepped out and headed in their direction.

"Bernice Wagner, meet Amanda Smith, our president. Bernie is Hilltop's new housekeeper."

Amanda smiled. "Welcome to our team."

"Thank you. I'm honored Erica chose me."

Erica escorted Bernie to her car then followed her partner into the kitchen.

Amanda tossed the truck key into the bowl. "Our new hire obviously passed the Millie test."

"Did she ever." Erica explained.

Amanda chuckled. "Now that you've taken care of business, are you ready for today's most important event?"

"I'll let you know in five hours." After changing shoes and donning a light-weight jacket, Erica placed her golf clubs in the truck's back seat.

Should she have accepted Brad's offer to pick her up? Too late to second-guess her decision now.

The closer Erica came to the Toccoa Hills golf club, the tighter she gripped the steering wheel. How would she and Brad react to seeing each other socially the first time since the accident? She pulled into the parking lot and spotted his fifteen-year-old SUV, then pulled her phone off the passenger seat and typed a text. "I'm here."

He responded. "Bringing golf cart to you."

Erica climbed out, removed her clubs from the back seat, and donned her golf visor. Brad pulled up behind the truck. She secured her clubs beside his then climbed in beside him. "Thanks for the chauffeur service."

"You're welcome." Brad gripped the steering wheel. "I need to tell you something before we head to the first nine."

Erica stole a sideways glance at his profile. "I'm listening."

"Most Saturday afternoons Jan and I played golf with Lauren and Carl Lowe." He paused as if fearing the gravity of his next words. "They're our closest friends."

"Why are you telling me this now?"

Brad hesitated. "They're waiting for us on the first tee."

"They're the reason you invited me to play today, aren't they?"

His eyes met hers. "Yes."

Erica's jaw tensed. "Why didn't you tell me we're a foursome before I drove all the way over here?"

"If I had told you ahead of time, would you have come?"

She broke eye contact. "Probably not."

"I apologize for blindsiding you. The truth is I want to share my entire world with you."

"You should have told me."

"I know." Brad grasped her hand, sending tingles racing through her limbs. "If you want to leave, I'll give them a logical excuse why you can't join us."

"Do they know I'm here?"

"Not yet."

Confusion muddled Erica's brain. Backing out at the last minute would embarrass Brad. If she stayed, how would Jan's closest friends react to the new woman in his life? "I'll stay."

"Lauren and Carl are two of the nicest people you'll ever meet." Brad squeezed her fingers then released her hand and drove past the clubhouse. He pointed to a couple standing beside a golf cart. "They're eager to meet you." Brad pressed his hand to her back as he escorted her toward the attractive couple. "Lauren and Carl, meet Erica Nelson."

The slender woman with a long dark ponytail sandwiched Erica's hand. "I've been so looking forward to meeting you and challenging these guys to a match."

Erica's eyes widened. "I've only been playing for a few months."

"Doesn't matter. We'll give you a handicap to balance the scores." Lauren released Erica's hand then looped her arm around her elbow. "You and I will ride together so we can become better acquainted and plan our game-winning strategy."

Overwhelmed by Lauren's warm greeting and take-charge attitude, Erica failed to summon enough courage to resist. Besides, maybe she'd learn more about Brad's late wife. After the guys switched clubs from one cart to the other, Erica climbed in beside Lauren. "How long have you known Brad?"

"The four of us have been friends most of our lives." She steered the cart toward the first tee. "After we all graduated from college, we returned to

Blue Ridge and renewed our friendships. We married within a few months of each other."

Erica swallowed. *Making me the awkward outsider.*

Lauren stepped out and pulled a club from her bag. "About today's game—" She shared tips while ambling to the first tee.

The guys teed off first, followed by Lauren. Daunted by her long drive, Erica stepped up and pushed her tee into the clay. She swung and missed the ball. Humiliation coupling with intimidation sent heat drifting from her neck to her cheeks.

Lauren moved closer. "Great practice swing. Now, drive that ball down the fairway and show the guys they're in for serious competition." She winked then backed away and stood between Brad and Carl.

Unwilling to let her partner down, Erica drew in a deep breath then slowly released the air. She lined up her driver and laser focused on the ball. The world around her stood still. She swung and drove the ball further down the fairway than ever before.

The men applauded. Lauren rushed onto the tee. "With shots like that, we're a cinch to win."

"What's the prize?"

"Bragging rights." She linked arms with Erica as they returned to the golf cart. After placing their clubs in their bags, Lauren climbed behind the wheel while Erica slid in beside her. "How long have you been playing golf?"

"My dad taught me when I was twelve." She drove onto the cart path. "Based on your second swing, you're a natural."

"If I ever learn to sink a putt on the first or second try."

"Putting is the toughest skill to master." Lauren braked beside Erica's ball. "I suggest you use your three-wood for this shot."

"Thanks for the tip." Erica climbed out, grabbed her club, and made her way onto the fairway. She aimed and swung. Pleased with her shot she returned to the golf cart. After continuing to drive shots down the fairway, they joined the guys on the first green. Miraculously, Erica had managed to land her ball four feet from the hole. She marked her spot then pocketed her ball and stepped back.

Both guys two-putted the hole. After sinking her ball with one stroke, Lauren moved close to Erica. There's a bit of a downhill curve, so aim slightly to the right of the hole."

"All right." Erica stepped onto the green and replaced the marker with her ball. She gripped her putter and aimed the head. *Here goes.* She tapped the ball with a light punch. The ball drifted right then turned and dropped into the hole.

Brad chuckled. "With your handicap, that putt puts you two ahead."

Lauren high-fived Erica. "Well done, partner."

After driving off the second tee, they returned to the golf cart. Erica glanced at Lauren's profile. "What do you and your husband do other than play golf?"

"Carl's a dentist. I teach high school English and creative writing. Brad told us you're a massage therapist and one of Hilltop Inn's owners."

What else had he told his friends about her? "I'm the chief executive officer."

"Impressive."

They chatted about their jobs and golf until they drove away beside the eighth tee and pulled up behind the guys. Brad and Carl selected clubs and strode onto the fairway. "Did Brad tell you his boys grew up with our sons?"

Erica shook her head.

"Jimmy's a good kid. It's a shame how one terrible decision resulted in a devastating accident."

"A few weeks after we moved to Blue Ridge, my daughter ran a stop sign. She was shaken to her core the day she appeared in court to face charges of texting while driving." Erica's eyes shifted to Brad driving his ball toward the green. "Ironic how ten months later she became a victim of another young person taking his eyes off the road."

"As a mother I understand your agony over Abby's injuries, especially knowing who caused the accident."

Had Brad told Lauren her daughter's name? Did she know about her emotional turmoil following the accident?

"Now that I've had a chance to learn a little about you, I need to tell you why it was my idea to invite you two to play with us. To begin, Jan was my best friend and Brad's first love. They dated all through high school and college. Watching her fight so hard then lose the battle to cancer devastated Brad. His heart shattered when she passed on to her eternal home. He quit playing golf. Carl and I tried to console him, to no avail. He refused invitations from friends and poured every ounce of energy into his sons and his job. Then he met you, and his heart began to mend."

Erica's eyes met Lauren's.

"I can only imagine your emotional turmoil." Lauren touched Erica's arm. "If you love Brad even half as much as he loves you, I pray you won't allow Jimmy's mistake to destroy your relationship with his father."

Tears erupted and flowed down Erica's cheeks. The woman she hadn't known existed an hour ago had touched her soul with her words. Were they enough to heal her internal conflict?

Chapter 25

Three days had passed since winning the golf match against Brad and Carl, and Erica hadn't told anyone about her interaction with Lauren. Maybe the opportunity would arise today. She made her way from Hilltop to the ranch house and walked into the kitchen. After dropping the inn's key into the bowl, she ambled to the den and sat at the table beside Awesam's president. "Bernie's third day on the job, and she and Millie are getting along as if they've been best friends for years."

"Thanks to you hiring a suspicion-proof housekeeper." Amanda turned her laptop toward Erica. "Check out the 'amenities' tab."

Erica tapped the keyboard, pulled up the list, and eyed the offerings. "Schedule a massage. Enjoy our sauna. Celebrate a special occasion. When did you finish the, 'request a private dining experience' tab?"

"Five minutes ago. I want your opinion."

Erica opened the tab and read the description. "Well done, except for one big problem. You've touted a chef award that doesn't exist."

"It won't be nonexistent for long."

Erica's brows furrowed. "What do you have up your sleeve?"

Amanda propped her arms on the table. "'Hilltop Inn's 'Holiday Dessert Competition' to take place the Saturday before Thanksgiving. We'll select participants and judges to guarantee Millie wins."

"How exactly does stacking the deck qualify as legitimate?"

"Simple. We'll introduce the competition as an annual event. Then next year we'll open the competition to the first ten people who sign up and enlist this year's winner as one of the judges."

"I have to admit your idea is creative." Erica pushed the laptop back to Amanda. "Millie will know this year is rigged."

"She won't care as long as she ends up with bragging rights. I have Wendy's approval. All I need is yours to put the event in motion."

"Considering we don't have another plan, I'll go along."

Abby wheeled in from the hall. "Another plan for what?"

Erica explained.

Abby chuckled. "Talk about an Awesam win. Millie's crazy request will end up creating great publicity for Hilltop. You have my vote."

"All right then."

Erica lifted off her chair. "Are you ready to car shop?"

"Oh yeah." Abby spun her wheelchair away from the table.

Erica grabbed her keys and purse off the kitchen counter then rushed to the foyer and opened the front door. After helping Abby into the truck and stowing the wheelchair, she slid behind the wheel and backed down to the street. How things had changed. A year ago, she worked part-time at a gift store and Abby was a high school senior who could drive her own car. A pain erupted in the back of Erica's throat. If she hadn't married the man she had first known as Brian Parker, they would still live in Asheville. She tightened her grip on the steering wheel. What it all boiled down to was Abby's accident was Gunter Benson's fault.

A deer wandered into the road.

Abby gasped.

Erica slammed on her brakes, missing the animal by inches.

"Quick reaction, Mom."

Erica's heart pounded in her chest as reality hit home. Except for the accident and nearly colliding with a deer, their lives were far better in Blue Ridge than they had been in Asheville and Baltimore. She eased the truck forward.

"I have a favor to ask—and don't take this the wrong way, Mom—I want to find the right car and negotiate the deal on my own."

"As an independent young woman who isn't allowing a wheelchair to interfere with her life, right?"

"Exactly." Abby fingered her seatbelt. "How'd your golf date go with Mr. Barkley?"

Erica stole a quick glance at her daughter. She had opened the door; it was time to walk through it. "We played eighteen holes with another couple."

"A double date."

"With Carl and Lauren Lowe, close friends of Brad and his wife."

"Ms. Lowe, my English teacher?"

Ah, that explained how Lauren knew her daughter's name. "Yes."

"She's a cool lady." Abby pointed toward the windshield. "Pull into that dealership."

"All right." Erica turned onto the property.

Moments after Erica helped her daughter out of the truck, a salesman rushed over and faced Erica. "Are you in the market for a new truck?"

"My daughter is your customer, sir, not me."

"I see." He eyed Abby. "Are you looking for a handicap-equipped vehicle, Miss...?"

"Nelson."

Erica cringed. Would her daughter ever drive a normal car again?

"This wheelchair is temporary." Abby squared her shoulders and lifted her chin. "I'm looking for a sedan with the following features."

Erica's mouth fell open as her daughter ticked off a long list of demands.

"In other words, don't waste my time showing me any cars other than what I'm looking for."

"Yes, ma'am." The wide-eyed salesman led the way to a row of pre-owned vehicles.

Erica followed at a distance, making it clear her daughter was in charge. After viewing a dozen cars, Abby wheeled to a sedan four years newer than the car Gunter had given her. "Here's what I'm willing to pay for this vehicle, and not one penny more."

"I'll speak to my manager and see what we can work out."

"There's nothing to work out. Either you take the deal, or I go to another dealership. And by the way, I'm paying cash."

The salesman cleared his throat. "I understand. However, I still need to talk to my manager. You're welcome to come inside and see our new models."

"Thanks, but we'll wait out here."

He pivoted and headed to the building.

"Well done." Erica high-fived her daughter. "Next year when Amanda and I shop for a new vehicle, we're taking you with us."

"Better yet, take Millie."

Erica chuckled. "Watching her and Amanda tag team to negotiate a deal would be fun."

"If they don't strangle each other." Abby nodded toward the show-room. "How long do you suppose our salesman will make us wait?"

"However long he thinks he'll need to break your resolve."

"In case he's watching us, let's give him a reason to speed up." Abby spun her chair around and wheeled to the truck.

Amanda followed and opened the passenger door.

The salesman dashed out of the building. "I've spoken to my manager, Miss Nelson, and we accept your offer."

"Excellent."

Erica closed the door and followed Abby into the building. After closing the deal and arranging to have the car delivered to their home, they drove to the Sweet Shoppe and bought cupcakes to celebrate Abby's victory.

Chapter 26

A thunderstorm ushering in the fifth day of November deepened Wendy's somber mood. Chris had spent November fourth dickering over jury selection before practicing his opening statement aloud with their stone fireplace as his backdrop. Today, for the first time, she would watch her husband plead a case in court.

While Chris stepped out of the shower, Wendy finished dressing then headed to the kitchen to prepare his breakfast. After adding vanilla creamer and sugar to her morning caffeine jolt, she removed a carton from the fridge. Images from Gunter's Las Vegas trial erupted as she cracked four eggs into a pan. That district attorney had won his case by proving the accused guilty beyond the shadow of a doubt. How would her husband defend Jimmy against a vindictive DA?

The moment Chris walked out of their bedroom, Wendy poured a mug of coffee and set it on the L-shaped counter. "One standard pre-trial breakfast coming up—two eggs over easy, dry toast, and black coffee."

He slid onto a stool and wrapped his fingers around the mug. "You're the most beautiful short-order cook on the planet."

Wendy smiled while dropping three slices of bread in the toaster. "I'm also the number one fan of the world's smartest courtroom lawyer." She grabbed a spatula and flipped the eggs over.

"From your lips to the jury's collective ears." Chris sipped his coffee.

"After you deliver your opening statement, they'll all agree with me." Wendy plated breakfast then settled beside Chris. After he blessed the food and prayed for guidance, Wendy spread butter on her toast. "What do you suppose the DA will say during his opening statement?"

"He'll attempt to befriend the jurors and play on their emotions, then explain the law and paint Jimmy as a menace to society."

"That's doesn't seem fair."

"Fairness is irrelevant. His job is to win his case." Chris bit a big chunk from his toast then ate the rest of his breakfast in silence. After swallowing his last bite and heading back to their suite, he returned and kissed her cheek then made his way to the garage.

Wendy ambled to the nursery and lifted her little guy from his crib. "Today I'm going to watch your brilliant daddy argue an important case while Grandma Linda takes care of you."

Ninety minutes after feeding Ryan, Wendy walked into the courtroom and slid into the back row beside Erica and Amanda. "Who'd have thought the three of us would sit together in a courtroom to watch another trial?"

Amanda crossed one leg over the other. "Except this time a real attorney will defend an innocent client."

"A brilliant defense attorney, mind you." Wendy craned her neck. "Is Brad here?"

Erica nodded. "He's sitting right behind Jimmy."

Wendy's focus shifted to the district attorney sitting at the prosecution table talking to a young man wearing a navy suit. Most likely an assistant DA.

Erica nudged Wendy and nodded toward a stunning young brunette wearing sunglasses sliding into the row across the aisle. "Do you recognize her?"

Wendy shook her head. "I've never seen her before."

The bailiff faced the audience. "All rise, the honorable Judge Elisabeth Davis presiding." The elegant middle-aged woman took her place on the bench.

Erica leaned close to Wendy. "What do you know about her?"

"Chris said she's one of the best."

The bailiff escorted six women and six men into the jury box then announced the case and introduced Christoper Armstrong as the defense attorney and DA Richard Watson as the prosecution.

"Here we go," whispered Emily.

The portly DA eased off his chair then skirted his table and meandered to the jury box. "Good morning, ladies and gentlemen. I hope y'all are comfortable." He moved close to the railing. "How many of y'all have children?"

Every juror raised a hand.

"Who among you has a teenager old enough to drive a car?"

Six jurors responded.

"Like me, you worry every time your son or daughter slides in behind the wheel, don't you?"

Nods.

"Today y'all will hear evidence against a young man whose conduct came this close—" He held his finger an inch from his thumb. "—to sending an eighteen-year-old girl in the prime of her life to an early grave—" He backed away from the jurors and thrust his arm toward the defense. "By a reckless young man who disregarded Georgia's law to satisfy his own selfish curiosity."

Watson turned back toward the jury. "Everyone knows it's against the law to hold a cell phone while driving and take one's eyes off the road to read a text. Right?" He paused. "The defendant is charged with reckless endangerment because his irresponsible behavior resulted in serious physical injury to an innocent young woman. Simply put, Mr. Barkley disregarded the law." The DA used exaggerated gestures. "While his foot remained on the accelerator, the defendant took his eyes off the road and focused all of his attention on a text message."

He sidled close to the railing. "At that moment a young woman who had braked at a four-way stop eased forward. While reading the message, the defendant blew through his stop sign and slammed into that young woman's car. As a result of his negligence, a severe spinal cord injury has relegated her to a wheelchair...possibly for the rest of her life."

Erica cringed. "Why is he exaggerating her injury?"

Wendy leaned close. "To score points. Chris will counter with his opening statement."

The DA sauntered from one end of the railing to the other while explaining the law. "Ladies and gentlemen, the state will prove the defendant disregarded the consequences of his actions, and that those consequences were foreseeable resulting in the criminal charge of reckless endangerment." He returned to his seat.

Chris stood. He moved across the courtroom and stopped three feet from the jury box. "Each of us has at one time or another been distracted and taken our eyes off the road." He paused appearing to make eye contact with each juror. "Perhaps by a flashy billboard or a new for-sale sign. Who wouldn't notice deer and her fawns grazing beside the woods or a dog running toward the road." Another pause. "Or a cell phone's ping. However, when Jimmy Barkley's phone pinged a text, he did not lift his phone off the passenger seat. He did not attempt to respond. Just as any of us might do, he simply took his eyes off the road."

Chris eased closer to the jurors. "The defense will prove this young man was unaware that the two-way stop had been changed to a four-way intersection. We will prove he slammed on the brakes the second he realized the pending danger. The district attorney would have you believe the other driver sustained injuries beyond repair. You will hear testimony to prove him wrong."

Chris placed his hands on the railing. "The young man, who had a perfect driving record before this unfortunate accident, took his eyes off the road for a brief moment. The same could be said about every other driver in this courtroom. Mr. Barkley did not act with willful disregard for the safety of others. He did not know his action could result in harm. In fact, ladies and gentlemen, we will prove Jimmy's split-second response saved a young woman's life." Chris strode away from the jurors and returned to his seat.

Drawing in deep, satisfying breaths, Wendy tapped Erica's arm. "Chris will win this case, and Abby will walk again."

Taking Wendy's comment to heart, the tension gripping Erica's neck eased until the district attorney called his first witness.

The sheriff who had broken the news about Abby's accident entered the courtroom and headed straight to the witness stand. For a half hour, Erica suffered through testimony about the accident. The damage to each vehicle. The road littered with broken glass and car parts. How the emergency crew pried her unconscious child from the wreckage and secured a neck brace to stabilize her spine.

When he finished, Chris approached the witness stand. "You were the first officer to arrive on the scene, correct?"

"Yes, sir."

"How soon after you arrived did the EMT's show up?"

"A matter of minutes."

"What happened after the injured drivers were transported to the hospital?"

"Two other deputies and I conducted a thorough investigation of the accident scene."

"When you examined the interior of Mr. Barkley's car, did you find his cell phone?"

The sheriff nodded. "It was on the floor in front of the passenger seat."

"Indicating his phone had been on the passenger seat at the time of the collision?"

"Correct."

"Did you discover evidence proving Mr. Barkley attempted to stop?"

"We did."

Chris faced the jury. "Describe what you found."

"Skid marks beginning three yards before the intersection and ending at the point of impact."

"What would have happened if Mr. Barkley hadn't applied his brakes?"

The sheriff turned toward the jury. "His car would have slammed into the driver's door. Based on the damage to the back half of the car, the driver most likely would not have survived."

Erica cringed.

"When did the county install a second set of stop signs at the intersection where the accident occurred?"

"Three months ago."

"During the time when Mr. Barkley lived in another state." Chris headed to the defense table. He removed items from a folder then returned to the witness stand and handed one to the witness. "This is a photograph of Mr. Barkley's view forty feet from the intersection. Tell me what you see."

The sheriff held the photo close. "A bush obscuring the stop sign."

"At this point would a driver unfamiliar with the recent change be aware of the upcoming stop?"

"No."

Chris held up the second photo. "This was taken at the spot where the new stop sign first comes into view, fifteen feet away." He stepped over to the jury box and handed the photos to the first juror then returned to the witness box. "Were you able to determine Mr. Barkley's speed?"

"Approximately forty-miles-per hour."

"What is the posted limit?"

"Forty-five."

"Given Mr. Barkley's obstructed view, by the time he saw the new stop sign and reacted, would he have been able to stop in time to avoid the collision?"

"Not a chance."

"Thank you." Chris returned to his seat.

Judge Davis leaned forward. "Do you want to cross, Mr. Watson?"

The DA conferred with his assistant then faced forward. "Not at this time."

"In that case, we'll take a lunch break and reconvene at one o'clock."

Wendy nudged Erica. "Score one for the brilliant defense attorney." She nodded toward the sunglasses-clad woman scurrying from the courtroom. "Maybe she's a reporter."

"Or a witness to the accident." Amanda uncrossed her legs. "How about we head over to Southern Charm for a quick lunch?"

Ninety minutes after exiting the courtroom, Erica settled beside Wendy and Amanda in the row they had vacated and motioned toward her left. "The mysterious brunette has returned."

"I still say she's here for the prosecution." Amanda set her purse on the seat. "I'm surprised the DA hasn't called Abby to testify."

Wendy silenced her cell phone. "He probably believes she'd do more to harm than help his case." The judge returned to the courtroom followed by the jury. "Here we go."

Watson called an accident expert to the stand. After the silver-haired man spent an agonizing hour answering questions and spouting mind-numbing statistics about incidents related to texting and driving, DA Watson returned to his desk.

Chris stood. "Did you examine the accident scene?"

"Only in photographs."

"I see." Chris plucked an item off the table then approached the witness and handed over the item. "Including this photo?"

The witness examined the picture. "I haven't seen this one."

"You're looking at the driver's view of the intersection from forty feet away. Given your expertise, would an obstructed view of a stop sign qualify as a mitigating circumstance in the resulting accident?"

"I'd have to say yes."

"Thank you." Chris returned to his seat.

The DA again chose not to cross. After the expert stepped down, Watson called Ashley Bowman to the stand.

Chris bolted to his feet. "Approach, Your Honor?"

Judge Davis motioned the attorneys forward while holding her hand over her microphone.

Erica leaned close to Wendy. "Do you have any idea what's going on?"

"Maybe she's not on the DA's witness list."

A minute passed. Chris returned to his table. Brad leaned forward as Chris spoke to his client.

The judge uncovered her mike. "The witness may approach the front."

The mysterious brunette stood and pushed her sunglasses to the top of her head then headed up the aisle.

Amanda peered around Erica. "I was right about her."

After swearing to tell the truth, the stunning young woman settled on the witness stand.

The DA swaggered over. "Where do you live, Ms. Bowman?"

"In an Atlanta suburb."

"What is your occupation?"

"I teach high school English."

"How do you know the defendant, Ms. Bowman?"

Ashley appeared to glance at the defense table. "We dated for little more than a year."

Erica gasped. "Oh my gosh, she's Jimmy's ex-girlfriend."

The DA shoved his hands in his pocket. "Were you an exclusive couple?"

Her chin dipped. "Yes."

"So, Mr. Barkley had every reason to believe your relationship would continue—"

"Objection. Calls for speculation."

"Sustained."

The DA pulled his hands from his pockets and gripped the witness-stand railing. "When did you break up with Mr. Barkley?"

"A few weeks ago," Ashley peered down and whispered her response.

Watson released his grip and stepped back. "Please answer aloud."

"A few weeks ago."

"Was Mr. Barkley upset—"

"Objection—"

The DA turned toward the judge. "Ms. Bowman's response goes to the defendant's state of mind, Your Honor."

"Counselor's objection is sustained. Rephrase your question, Mr. Watson."

He faced his witness. "What was Mr. Barkley's reaction when you told him your relationship was over?"

"He um…"

"He who?"

"Jimmy—" Ashley's voice quivered. "—didn't want to break up."

"Who can blame him? You're a beautiful young woman."

"Objection, the district attorney is testifying, Your Honor."

"Sustained." The judge leaned toward the witness box. "Move along, Counselor."

Watson stepped closer to Ashley. "Following your rejection, did you communicate with Mr. Barkley?"

She hesitated. "Not until I sent him a text."

"The day of the accident."

"Yes."

"Adding to the defendant's anxiety—" Watson spun away and flicked his hand over his shoulder. "Withdrawn." He returned to his seat.

Chris appeared to speak to Jimmy then stood. "What did you text to Mr. Barkley the day of the accident?"

"A picture of us."

"With a comment?"

"No."

"Which means a quick glance was all he needed to know who sent it."

"I suppose."

"Did he respond?"

"Not yet."

Chris turned toward the defense table as if making eye contact with Jimmy.

Erica nudged Wendy. "What's he doing?"

"Thinking."

Chris spun back toward Ashley. "How many times during the past year have you ridden in the car while Jimmy was behind the wheel?"

Ashley shrugged. "Fifty? Sixty?"

"Did you ever see him text while driving?"

She shook her head. "Never."

"Do you consider him a safe driver—"

"Objection."

"Overruled."

Ashley turned toward the jury. "Jimmy Barkley is the safest driver I know."

"Thank you, Ms. Bowman." Chris returned to his seat.

The judge leaned close to her mike. "Do you wish to redirect, Counselor?"

The DA stood. "Yes, Your Honor."

"Go ahead."

Watson moved toward the witness. "Why did you end your relationship with the defendant?"

"Objection, Your Honor. Irrelevant."

"The witness's answer is relevant to the defendant's character."

"I'll allow the question. Go ahead and answer, Ms. Bowman."

"I...um...thought I needed a break." Ashley paused and turned toward the jury. "Until I realized I could date a hundred different guys and never find anyone as thoughtful and caring as Jimmy Barkley."

Wendy held her hand in front of her mouth and leaned close to Erica. "If I'm not mistaken, the DA just made a case-losing mistake."

Watson spun away from the witness. "The prosecution rests, Your Honor."

Judge Davis faced Ashley. "You may step down, Ms. Bowman. Court is adjourned until nine a.m. tomorrow." The judge rapped her gavel.

Ashley headed straight to the row behind the defense table.

The moment the jury filed out, Jimmy spun toward Ashley.

Wendy nudged Erica. "Are you gonna find out what's going on between those two?"

The last thing Jimmy and his dad needed was one more person adding to the drama. "I'll wait for Brad to reach out to me."

Chapter 27

Eager to watch her husband in action, Wendy entered the courtroom fifteen minutes before the trial was scheduled to begin. She eased into the last row and typed a text to Erica. "Where are you?"

"Two minutes away."

Wendy responded with a thumbs-up emoji then scanned the room. Chris and Jimmy huddled at the defense table. Brad and Ashley sat beside each other in the row behind them. The district attorney strode up the aisle and set his briefcase on the prosecution table. His assistant followed. Would the trial end today or continue into tomorrow? As usual on a night before arguing a case, Chris had closed himself in their home office until bedtime. Respecting his need to focus every ounce of energy on the trial, Wendy had left him alone this morning after preparing his breakfast.

"Hey." Erica scooted into the row, followed by Amanda.

Wendy silenced her phone. "Did you talk to Brad last night?"

Erica nodded.

Wendy stared at her partner's profile. "And?"

"Ashley texted the picture because she wanted to resume her relationship with Jimmy. Now she blames herself for the accident."

Amanda crossed a leg over her knee. "Rightfully so."

The bailiff entered the courtroom. After announcing the judge and ushering in the jury, he called the session to order.

Chris stood. "The defense calls Dr. Arthur Kennedy to the stand."

Abby's doctor headed up the aisle. After swearing to tell the truth, he settled on the witness stand.

Chris moved to the front of the defense table. "Are you the neurologist treating Abby Nelson, the young woman who was injured in the accident?"

"I am."

"Describe the young woman's injuries for the jury."

The doctor relayed details, explaining the difference between a complete and incomplete spinal-cord injury.

"Based on her condition, what is Miss Nelson's long-term prognosis?"

"With time and therapy, she has better than a sixty-percent chance of a full recovery."

"Meaning she'll likely walk again."

"Yes, sir."

Wendy nudged Erica. "Did you know Abby's potential outcome is that positive?"

"Not until now."

Chris lifted an item off the desk and carried it to the witness stand. "Based on this photograph, what would have happened if Mr. Barkley's car had hit the driver's door?"

Dr. Kennedy studied the picture. "If she had survived, chances are the impact would have broken her neck and paralyzed her."

"Objection, calls for speculation."

"The witness is an expert on spinal-cord injuries, Your Honor."

"Overruled."

Chris faced the witness. "Based on the photograph and your experience, did Mr. Barkley's quick action to slam on his brakes save a young woman from death or life as a possible quadriplegic?"

"Absolutely."

"Thank you." Chris returned to his seat.

The judge faced the prosecution table. "Do you want question the witness?"

Watson held up a finger and leaned close to his assistant.

The young man stood, remaining behind the desk. "Based on your testimony, the victim faces better than a thirty-percent chance of remaining wheelchair bound for the rest of her life, correct?"

"For the moment. However, with each therapy session, her chances for a full recovery increase."

"No more questions." The assistant dropped onto his seat.

After the neurologist stepped down, Chris called Dr. Abernathy to the stand.

Wendy tapped Erica. "Do you know him?"

She shook her head.

Chris approached the witness stand. "Were you the physician who treated Mr. Barkley immediately after the accident?"

"I was."

"What was his demeanor when the EMTs brought him to the emergency room?"

"He was distraught and repeatedly asked about the woman in the other car. He begged us to tell her how sorry he was."

"What was your first action after reading the X-rays of Mr. Barkley's right leg?"

"I contacted an orthopedic surgeon."

"Why didn't you simply cast his broken leg?"

"Repairing the extensive damage to three bones required surgery." He described the fractures in detail.

"How many accident victims have you treated as an ER physician?"

"Hundreds."

"Based on your experience, would applying pressure to a brake pedal during impact cause the serious injuries you observed on the x-rays?"

"Without a doubt."

"Mr. Barkley's heroic attempt to avoid an accident left him seriously injured. Withdrawn. Thank you, Doctor."

DA Watson declined to question the doctor.

Moments after the ER physician left, Chris called his next witness. After the bailiff swore him in, he approached the elderly gentleman. "Your home is one lot away from the intersection where the accident occurred, correct?"

"Yes, sir."

"Where were you moments before the collision?"

"Sitting on my front porch reading a book."

"Describe what you heard and saw?"

"Well, sir, I looked up the second I heard brakes screeching. I know that sound. That driver did everything possible to stop—"

"Objection, the witness has no way of knowing what the driver was or wasn't attempting to do."

"Sustained."

Chris moved closer to the white-haired gentleman. "What did you observe after you heard screeching brakes?"

"The car attempting to brake slammed into the other car. That's when I called 911."

"How many accidents have occurred at that intersection?"

"At least a dozen. Two after the county installed those extra stop signs. I've called the authorities more than once about cutting down that bush in front of the stop sign. Maybe now someone will listen."

"We can hope." Chris turned toward the jury. He paused then returned to his seat. After the DA again declined to cross-examine the witness, Chris turned to say something to Brad and Jimmy.

Erica fidgeted. "What do you suppose the three of them are talking about?"

Wendy's eyes remained trained on her husband as her mind drifted to a conversation the night Brad hired him to defend Jimmy. "Probably whether or not to allow Jimmy to testify."

Amanda uncrossed her legs. "If you ask me, Chris has already established Jimmy's innocence, so why would he expose him to the DA's cross?"

Wendy's focus shifted to the jury box. "No matter how careful attorneys are in selecting the jury during voir dire, jurors are unpredictable."

Amanda chuckled. "Now you sound like a lawyer."

"You'd be surprised how much I've learned sharing a home office with my brilliant husband."

Chris rose. "The defense calls James Barkley to the stand."

Silence hung heavy as the young man lifted his crutches off the floor and clomped his way to the stand. His sports jacket stood in stark contrast to the shorts he wore, which exposed his foot-to-thigh cast on his right leg at a slight bent-knee angle. After swearing to tell the truth, he stepped into the witness box and propped his crutches against the railing.

Chris pointed to the defense table. "Brad Barkley, who's sitting in the first row, is your father. Did you, your brother, and our district attorney's son all attend the same high school where Mr. Barkley is principal?"

"We did."

Chris moved closer to Jimmy. "You lost your mother to cancer a little more than three years ago?"

"Yes, I still miss her."

"She was an incredible lady. After you graduated from the University of Georgia with a business degree two years ago, where did you accept a job?"

"In the Atlanta area."

"Having lived away from Blue Ridge for all that time, were you aware of the additional stop signs at the intersection where the accident occurred?"

"No. The day of the accident was the first time I had driven on that road after I came back to town to spend a few weeks with my dad."

"When you first climbed into your car that day, where did you put your cell phone?"

"On the passenger seat."

Chris turned toward the jury. "Was the phone still on the seat when you heard the ping?"

"Yes."

"Tell the jury what happened from that moment."

Jimmy angled his shoulders toward the jury. "First I glanced at the screen for a second then focused back on the road. The new stop sign came into view the exact same time the other car began to move into the intersection. I slammed on my brakes, praying I could stop in time." Jimmy's voice quivered. "I couldn't."

"Would you have noticed the new stop sign sooner if you hadn't glanced at your cell phone?"

"No. I've played the accident over and over in my mind. I'll never forget the terrible crunch of metal and shattering glass when my face slammed into the airbag. My leg was trapped in the wreckage, so I couldn't reach my phone or climb out and help the other driver." Jimmy swiped his fingers across his cheeks. "I would give my life if I could go back, stay home, or take a different route."

Wendy leaned forward and scanned the jurors' faces. Two women dabbed their eyes.

Chris placed his hands on the witness-stand railing. "Do you need to take a break?"

Jimmy shook his head.

"Following the accident did you visit the injured young woman?"

He nodded. "We were in the same hospital. The day after my surgery, my dad and I went to her room so I could tell her how sorry I was for what happened."

"How did she react?"

"She said she forgave me because she understood the accident wasn't my fault."

"Objection. Calls for speculation."

"Sustained."

"I'll rephrase. Did the young woman you injured blame you for the accident?"

"No. I pray every day for God to heal her. I know one day she'll walk again."

Erica dabbed at the tears spilling down her cheeks. "You're a good person, Jimmy," she whispered.

Wendy grasped Erica's hand.

"Thank you, for showing the jury your character, Jimmy." Chris pivoted then returned to his seat.

The judge turned toward the prosecution. "Do you wish to cross, Counselor?"

He remained silent for a long moment as if debating his next move. "No."

Chris stood. "The defense rests, Your Honor."

"Ladies and gentlemen, we'll reconvene in one hour for summations." Judge Davis tapped her gavel.

Amanda scooted to the edge of her seat. "Jimmy's testimony touched every person on the jury."

Following a quick lunch, the Awesam partners returned to the courthouse. Ashley sat alone on a bench outside the courtroom. Wendy looped her hand around Erica's elbow. "We should go talk to her."

Erica stared at her as if she'd grown a third eye. "She doesn't have a clue who we are."

"She will when we introduce ourselves." Wendy withdrew her hand then headed straight to the bench. "Hi. I'm Wendy, Chris Armstrong's wife." She aimed her thumb over her shoulder. "These two ladies are my business partners and closest friends. Amanda is Abby's mother and Erica is Brad's friend."

The stunning brunette's gaze crept from one to the other. "Last night I saw a picture of you on an end table in the Barkleys' living room." Her eyes flicked back to Wendy. "What's the chance Mr. Armstrong will win Jimmy's case?"

"Based on the jury's reaction to Jimmy, I'm guessing better than ninety percent."

"The ten percent is what scares me." The young woman's eyes cast downward. "Jimmy doesn't deserve any of this. Neither does Abby."

Wendy smiled at Ashley. "Your testimony helped big time."

"I hope you're right." Ashley glanced at her watch. "It's almost time."

The partners followed the young woman into the courtroom. Ashley headed to the seat behind the defense table while they returned to the back row. Wendy slid in beside Awesam's CEO. "Did you know about your photo in Brad's house?"

"Not until two minutes ago." Erica nodded toward the jurors filing in.

Moments after the bailiff called the court to order, Chris eased off his seat and moved toward the jury box. "Reckless endangerment requires proof a defendant acted in a way that showed a complete disregard for the consequences of his actions, and that those consequences were foreseeable. Let's examine what experts and witnesses have revealed about the accident." He stopped in front of the first juror. "The stop sign, which was installed while Mr. Barkley lived in Atlanta, was hidden from his view by a tall bush until his car was ten feet from the intersection."

Chris moved to the second juror. "Mr. Barkley was driving under the posted speed limit." He stepped in front of juror number three. "The sheriff, who's an accident expert, explained how skid marks proved Jimmy did everything humanly possible to avoid the accident."

He stepped back and appeared to scan the jurors. "DA Watson would have you believe a split-second glance at a cell phone sitting on the passenger seat proves this innocent young man totally disregarded the consequences of his action." Chris moved further along the railing. "How long does it take to glance in a rearview mirror? One second? Two? At forty miles per hour, a car travels approximately fifty feet per second. Every time you check the cars behind, do you risk an accident? Of course, you don't."

He paused and placed his hands on the railing in front of the fourth juror—one of the women who had wiped away tears during Jimmy's testimony. "The truth is—" Chris aimed his arm toward the defense table. "That young man's quick response prevented him from t-boning the driver's door and snuffing out a young woman's life."

The juror nodded.

Chris dropped his arm to his side. "Even if Jimmy's cell phone hadn't pinged a text, the stop sign did not become visible from the road in time for him to stop." He backed away from the railing. "Ladies and gentlemen, find James Barkley not guilty of this erroneous charge to tell the prosecution the state has failed to prove this erroneous and vindictive charge." Chris spun away from the jury and returned to the defense table.

Amanda nudged Wendy's arm. "Your brilliant husband nailed his closing statement."

Wendy's chest puffed. "Like a champ."

DA Watson slowly lifted off his chair and ambled toward the jurors, as if Chris's closing statement weighed heavy on his shoulders. He stopped five feet from the railing. "It is against the law to read, write, or send text messages while driving. If the defendant hadn't taken his eyes off the road, he might have seen the stop sign a second sooner and had enough time to avoid slamming into an innocent victim."

Watson buttoned his jacket over his portly frame. "Ladies and gentlemen, you must convey an important lesson to every young person in North Georgia by holding the defendant responsible for his actions." He returned to his chair.

Amanda scoffed. "Talk about a weak closing argument."

Wendy nodded. "He knows his case is toast."

After the judge relayed instructions to the jury, the bailiff led them out of the courtroom.

Erica scooted to the edge of the seat. "Abby wants to be in the courtroom to hear the verdict."

"Based on my husband's brilliant defense and the jury's reaction during closing arguments, I predict they'll return a not-guilty verdict before suppertime. I suggest you pick Abby up, so we can hang out at Mountain Mama's new location and wait for Chris's call."

Amanda nodded. "Great idea."

Erica called Abby, then drove straight to the crisis center. After stashing her daughter's wheelchair in the trunk, she headed to town. During the short drive she toplined Chris's defense.

After they arrived at the coffee lounge, Abby maneuvered into her wheelchair. Erica helped her over the curb then held the door open. Abby wheeled her chair between Amanda and Wendy. "According to Mom, Chris delivered a skillful defense and closing argument. I wish I could have watched the trial, but I understand why Chris didn't want the jury to see me as a victim."

"Defending a client is all about strategy. Now that Jimmy's case is in the jury's hands, I think it's okay to tell you the underlying reason the DA charged him." Wendy craned her neck to scan the lounge, then leaned over the table. "Two years ago, Brad expelled Watson's son from school for selling drugs. As a result, he was kicked off the football team and lost a college scholarship."

Amanda snapped her fingers. "That's why Chris called the case erroneous and vindictive."

Wendy tilted her head. "Exactly."

Erica drummed her fingers. "If you ask me, voters need to suspend the DA during the next election."

"Someone will have to run against him for that to happen—" Wendy leaned back. "And that person definitely won't be Chris." Following another hour of discussion about the trial, Wendy's phone pinged a text. "The jury's reached a verdict. Court reconvenes in thirty minutes." She pocketed her phone. "Amanda and I will meet you two at the courthouse."

After rushing out of the coffee lounge to drive to the courthouse, Erica and her daughter headed up the aisle to the row behind Brad and Ashley. Abby shifted her body onto the bench, glanced at the row in front of her, then held her hand in front of her mouth and whispered, "Is she's Jimmy's ex-girlfriend?"

Erica nodded as the bailiff escorted the jury into the courtroom.

Judge Davis faced the jurors. "Has the jury arrived at a verdict?"

The foreman stood and held up a sheet of paper. "We have, Your Honor."

The judge motioned to the bailiff who delivered the paper to her. She quickly read the paper before returning it to the foreman. "How does the jury find in the case of Georgia against James Barkley?"

"We find the defendant not guilty."

The Awesam partners high-fived each other.

Brad leaned over the railing and clapped one hand on Chris's shoulder and the other on his son's.

Ashley broke down in tears.

Erica's daughter lifted herself onto her wheelchair and wheeled beside the front row. "Ashley, I'm Abby Nelson."

The stunning brunette scooted to the end of the row. "I'm so sorry."

"From what I've heard, Chris proved the accident was the county's fault, not yours or Jimmy's."

"If I hadn't broken up with him, he wouldn't have been here."

"Who knows? He might have taken a notion to visit his dad. Besides, you're here now, and Jimmy's been proven innocent. That's what counts."

Amanda touched Erica's arm. "Abby is an amazing young woman."

Erica dabbed her eyes. "Yeah, I know."

Brad peered over his shoulder. "Your husband is a brilliant attorney, Wendy."

Wendy's chest puffed. "Yes, he is."

His eyes crept to Erica. "I'm glad you're here."

"So am I."

Chapter 28

Four afternoons after the trial, Amanda climbed onto a tall stepladder in Hilltop's living room and placed the top section of the artificial, nine-foot spruce Christmas tree in place while Erica steadied the ladder. "We were smart not to include this tree and all your decorations in your Asheville estate sale."

"Same thing I was thinking about the gorgeous wreath and garland you brought from New Orleans."

"Those date back to my life with Preston." Amanda climbed off the stepladder. "We need to make sure the lights are working."

"I'm on it." Erica plugged the electrical cord into the socket, illuminating hundreds of miniature white lights. "So far we're batting a thousand." She unplugged the lights then opened the last of four large plastic containers revealing an array of blue and gold ornaments in a variety of shapes and sizes.

"Did you and Brad make any decisions about your relationship last night?"

"We did." Erica removed a spool of four-inch-wide gold and white wired ribbon from a container then carried the ribbon to the tree.

"What'd you decide?"

"To pick up where we left off before the accident." Erica climbed onto the tall ladder. "He's my date for tonight's big event."

"Any update on the Ashley and Jimmy saga?"

"Seems they're a couple again, although she's still struggling with guilt over the accident. Ashley took a leave of absence from her job so she can stay here until Jimmy's leg heals."

"Then what?"

"They have no idea." Erica secured the ribbon close to the treetop then wrapped ribbon around the tree twice. "I need your help." She tossed the spool to Amanda. When they finished wrapping ribbon around the tree and tucking sections into the branches, Erica decorated the tree top with large blue and gold flowers and a pair of white doves. As she climbed down from the ladder, the front door swung open.

Millie dashed in and set a box on the coffee table. "Fancy garland and wreath on the front door."

Amanda brushed a lock of hair away from her face. "My only contribution to Hilltop's Christmas décor."

"I brought the perfect decorations for our fireplace. Twelve different candlesticks. Instead of displaying candles—" Millie pulled an item from the box and removed the bubble wrap. "Each one holds an ornament."

Erica eyed the elegant gold ornament nestled in the crystal candle holder. "Talk about creative."

"Wait 'til you see the rest." Millie unwrapped the remaining eleven. After arranging all twelve on the mantel, she stepped back. "What do you think?"

"Hmm." Erica stepped beside Millie. "They're elegant and eye-catching. In fact, you should help us finish trimming the tree, right, Amanda?"

"Why not."

Millie propped her hands on her hips. "What's with those flowers on top of the tree instead of an angel or a star?"

"Hold on." Erica grabbed a handful of gold sticks glued with miniature stars, then climbed up and arranged them as if they were sparkly fireworks exploding from the floral display. "Now what's your opinion?"

"Still strange, but better." Millie lowered her arms and plucked an ornament from a container. "Why'd you pick these colors?"

"They worked well in my Asheville living room."

"A color-coordinated Christmas tree. Interesting."

An hour after Millie hung the first ornament, Erica wrapped the quilted gold skirt around the tree stand, then stood and stepped back to admire their work. "Perfect."

Millie nodded. "I have to admit I like your tree topper, even though it's not traditional."

Amanda guffawed. "Talk about untraditional. You hot glued ornaments into twelve candle holders."

"Yeah, well." Millie repositioned two of the candlesticks. "If you ask me, Hilltop's den needs a more Christmasy tree. Maybe I should buy one and donate all my decorations."

"Umm." Amanda cleared her throat. "You don't need to—"

Millie scoffed. "You're afraid my decorations are tacky as all get-out, aren't you?"

"The thought did cross my mind."

"I'll show you." Millie spun toward Erica. "I need to borrow your truck."

"Why?"

"To drive to Walmart and buy the biggest tree they have." Hilltop's chef grabbed the empty box and scurried out the front door.

Erica popped the lid onto a container. "Are you worried about Millie's taste?"

"Heck no, but I'm not about to compliment her until after her tree's up and decorated."

"Are you saying you gave her a hard time to goad her into taking immediate action?"

"Excellent observation, Sherlock. Now what do you say we take all these empty containers next door and talk more about you and Brad."

"The containers? Yeah. The conversation? Not a chance."

As Chris turned onto his parents' driveway leading to their two-story home, Wendy gazed at the miniature white lights framing the high-pitched roof. Accent lighting illuminated the stone-and-brick façade and front door draped with lighted garland. "Did your parents hire a professional decorator?"

"Only for the exterior." Chris climbed out then dashed to the passenger side and opened both doors. Wendy stepped onto the concrete while her husband lifted his son from the car carrier.

"It's sweet of your mom to invite us for dinner."

"She's more excited about seeing her grandson than the two of us."

"Who can blame her? He's adorable." Wendy looped her hand around Chris's elbow as they made their way to the covered front porch. He rang the bell.

Linda pulled the door open. "There's my sweet grandbaby."

Chris placed Ryan in his mother's arms then helped Wendy slip out of her coat. "Something smells delicious."

"Come on in, and your dad will pour us some wine."

Chris tossed her coat onto the living room sofa, then pressed his hand on Wendy's back as they headed to the back of the house.

Shouts of surprise and enthusiastic applause erupted as they entered the massive combination kitchen and family room. Amanda, Erica, Brad, and Millie stood along the back of the L-shaped sectional sofa facing a floor-to-ceiling, stone fireplace draped with a 'Happy Birthday, Wendy' banner. Tommy stood beside Abby's wheelchair in front of the French doors leading to the deck overlooking downtown Blue Ridge.

"Oh my gosh." Wendy pressed her hand to her chest as happy tears pooled. "No one has ever surprised me with a birthday party."

Chris's grandmother, Susan, rushed over. "It's about time someone celebrated your special day, honey."

Chris slid his arm around his grandmother's' shoulders. "Grandma and Mom coordinated this shindig."

Susan nodded toward her granddaughter. "With a little help from your sister and brother-in-law."

As if on cue, Allison waddled over with one hand looped around her husband's arm and the other pressed to her eight-month baby bulge. Mark patted his wife's hand. "Fortunately, none of Allison's patients are in labor tonight."

Susan nodded. "Thank goodness, because Dr. Baker has no business delivering babies this close to bringing our family's second grandchild and first granddaughter into this world." She placed her hand on Allison's belly. "If I were a betting woman, I'd lay odds on Allison delivering at least a week early."

"I wouldn't underestimate a retired obstetric nurse's prediction." Keith handed his son and daughter-in-law glasses of white wine. "Happy birthday, Wendy."

"Thank you." She smiled at Chris's dad and law firm partner. "I can't believe ten months have passed since I first met you and asked Linda to help me find my father." Memories of the moment she and Chris met Douglas

Hewitt at his Hilton Head home played in her mind. His dismissal when he claimed her mother had been a one-night stand. His offhand comment that he'd been a dumb college kid who'd had too much to drink. "I don't care if he ever contacts me because I have the best father-in-law in the world."

Keith clasped his hand on Chris's shoulder. "You married an astute young woman."

Chris winked at Wendy. "She's also beautiful and smart."

"Well, I do declare." Wendy crossed her hands on her chest and poured on her best Mississippi accent. "All this flattery is likely to make me blush like a sweet little ole southern belle."

Keith burst out laughing. "Maybe you should have defended Jimmy against our infamous district attorney."

Susan chuckled. "Wendy would charm the socks off any jury."

Linda wandered in from the kitchen and linked arms with Wendy. "Tonight, you're Queen Wendy, and all your subjects are going to serve you." Her mother-in-law led her to a recliner angled toward the sofa. The same chair Wendy had occupied during her surprise combo wedding and baby shower six months earlier.

Wendy's heart filled with joy as the people she loved most in the world gathered to celebrate her twenty-fourth birthday. Life couldn't be better.

Chapter 29

T he Saturday before Thanksgiving, Erica and Amanda draped the 'Hilltop Inn's Holiday Dessert Competition' banner above the dining room entrance. When finished, Erica stepped off the ladder and eyed Amanda. "Kudo's for convincing Gail Weston to cover our event."

Amanda climbed down and folded her ladder. "I promised her an invitation to our holiday open house and an exclusive on next year's event."

Bernie placed a floral centerpiece on the table. "Who's Gail Watson?"

"A reporter who befriended us earlier this year."

"Befriended is a major understatement." Millie placed her chocolate peppermint cake beside an apple pie. "She's the reporter who rescued my partners from Gunter Benson's vicious lies."

Amanda pivoted toward Millie, her jaw clenched.

Seconds after Bernie returned to the kitchen, Millie pulled Amanda close to the window. "I know that look. You think I blabbed too much, don't you?"

Amanda folded her arms across her chest. "Didn't you?"

Millie turned her back toward the kitchen door. "First of all, Bernie listened to Nancy's podcast last spring when she interviewed the three of you, so she already knew how you inherited this place, and that Gunter had deceived you. For your information, I didn't breathe a word about the three of you being married to the scumbag." She shrugged. "Although, chances are Bernie has drawn her own conclusions."

Amanda tapped her fingers on her arms. "With a little help from our loquacious CIO who's charged with gathering, not disseminating information."

"Your fancy word for chatty doesn't change the facts. You didn't think I knew what loquacious meant, did you?"

"If the description fits—"

"Enough already." Erica's eyes snapped from Amanda to Millie. "In forty minutes, we're hosting a competition to crown you queen of holiday desserts. So, I suggest you two make nice with each other."

Millie huffed as she spun away from Amanda. "I'd win even if you hadn't rigged the competition."

Bernie wandered in carrying a large tray—her eyes wide.

Assuming their housekeeper had heard, Erica nudged Millie's arm. "The next time you admit the truth, you might want to lower your voice."

"No need." Bernie set a tray on the table. "Millie already told me."

Wendy breezed in from the front porch and placed a cake on the table. "Allison's entry is guaranteed to lose, even if this was a real competition."

A second of silence ensued, followed by laughter.

Erica looped her arm around Wendy's elbow. "Perfect timing." She explained.

Bernie waved a dismissive hand. "You ladies don't need to worry about me letting the cat out of the litter box. Millie swore me to secrecy. Next year *I'll* enter a dessert." She transferred a chocolate pie and a plate of decorated sugar cookies from the tray to the table. "Does whoever baked the entries know they won't win?"

Wendy nodded. "They're also sworn to secrecy."

Bernie placed a card with a number in front of each dessert. "Working with you ladies is a hoot and a half."

The doorbell rang. Erica pointed to the ladders. "Amanda, you and Wendy put those away while I answer the door." She hastened to the foyer and pulled the door open to see Gail. "We're delighted you're covering Hilltop's inaugural holiday competition." She escorted the reporter into the living room.

"You and your partners continue to amaze me." Gail snapped a series of photos while interviewing Amanda about the competition and the inn.

At two o'clock Hilltop guests gathered in the dining room as Amanda introduced the judges—Chris's grandmother, a Sweet Shoppe chef, and the Armstrong law firm receptionist.

Beginning with Allison's entry, Erica and Bernie placed small samples on three plates. The judges tasted and talked amongst themselves, then moved on to the next dessert. After sampling the final entry, the judges huddled in the living room while the guests speculated which dessert would win.

Susan led her cohorts back into the dining room. "Before we announce the winner, I want to commend Hilltop's owners for creating this competition to showcase our town's culinary talents. While every entry deserves praise, one stands out as a clear winner." Susan moved to the end of the table. "Dessert number five, chocolate peppermint cake."

"Oh, my goodness." Millie crossed her palms on her chest. "I can't believe I won."

Erica suppressed a giggle as the guests applauded and showered Millie with accolades. Had any of them or Gail suspected two of the judges were in on the deal?

Amanda lifted a plaque off the sideboard and presented it to Millie. "Monday we'll have your name engraved as the first winner of 'Hilltop

Inn's Holiday Dessert Competition.' As part of your reward, we invite you to be one of our next year's judges."

"I'd be honored."

Gail photographed and interviewed Millie, while the partners and Bernie served the desserts to Hilltop's guests—their reward for attending the event. After all the guests and two of the judges left, Susan lifted Millie's plaque off the table. "Am I free to share the real skinny about today's vote?"

"You might as well." Amanda shrugged. "Bernie's enlightened."

"All right." Susan fingered the engraving. "Even though I understood the reason for today's event, I worried about fudging the results—that it wouldn't appear as credible." She set the plaque on the table. "As it turned out, our Sweet Shoppe chef, who was the only judge with any real credibility, voted hands down for Millie's cake. Even better, my son and grandson's receptionist and I agreed that Millie's was the best."

Hilltop's chef snapped her fingers. "I told you I would have won even if the competition hadn't been rigged."

Bernie tapped Millie's arm. "I believe 'predetermined' is a much better word to describe today's competition."

Amanda dug her fork into a slice of chocolate peppermint cake. "If we had trusted our chef's culinary abilities, maybe we wouldn't have needed an underhanded outcome."

Millie stared wide-eyed at Awesam's president. "Are you suffering from a fever or a guilty conscience?"

"Neither." Amanda swallowed a bite then aimed her fork at Millie. "I'm simply stating the facts."

"Know what, Millie?" Susan lifted the plaque and moved to Millie's side. "We need to excuse these young whippersnappers for underestimating us senior citizens and decide where to hang your well-deserved award."

"I know the perfect spot." Bernie dashed into the living room and pointed to the wall behind the book stand. "Right there."

Millie followed. "Hmm. When Erica, Wendy, even Amanda welcome new guests and tell them about Hilltop's scrapbook, they'll remember to brag about the inn's award-winning chef."

"Smart move, Bernie." Wendy pulled her phone from her back pocket. "Oh my gosh." Her eyes widened. "Allison's in labor."

Chapter 30

Thanksgiving morning the air dipped to the lowest temperature since autumn had blown into Blue Ridge. Wendy set her coffee mug on an end table before pulling a French door open. A blast of cold air whipped her hair and sent a shiver racing through her limbs. Duke bounded back inside and sprawled in front of the fireplace. A giggle escaped as she gripped her mug.

Chris sauntered in cuddling Ryan in his arms. "What do you suppose tickled your mommy's funny bone this morning?"

Wendy faked a shiver. "I was imagining your great-great-grandmother cursing freezing-cold mornings before someone invented indoor plumbing."

Chris placed their son in Wendy's arms. "Where's your mommy's pioneer spirit?"

"As if your daddy would prefer hitching a horse to a wagon to take us to Grandma's house instead of cranking up all those horses under the hood." Wendy settled on a chair beside the fire. "Although, if we were living in the nineteenth century, he would've shot a big turkey for our Thanksgiving dinner."

Chris chuckled while heading to the kitchen area. "Lucky for Grandma Linda, today's bird was pre-plucked and purchased ready to stuff and bake."

Wendy nuzzled her little guy's neck. "In a few hours, you'll experience your first Thanksgiving and meet your new cousin, Ellie." Duke yawned, then lifted off his belly and licked Ryan's foot, triggering a giggle.

Chris grabbed Wendy's ringing phone off the counter and slid his finger across the screen. "Hey, Kayla." He carried the phone to Wendy then sat on the sofa and propped his feet on the coffee table.

Wendy smiled at her half-sister. "Happy Thanksgiving, sis."

"Thanks. How's my little cousin doing?"

"See for yourself." Wendy held the phone in front of her son's face. "Say hi to your Aunt Kayla."

Ryan reached for the phone while greeting his aunt with a babble.

Kayla's face lit up with a smile. "He's a sweetie."

"Ryan loves his Nashville aunt." Wendy raised her phone. "Any new updates on your mother?"

"Some days she seems better, others not so much." Kayla's smile evaporated. "Mom and Dad didn't want to spend all day cooking, so we're going out for dinner. What about you and Chris?"

"We'll celebrate with the family at his parents' house."

"Sounds like fun." Kayla fell silent for a long moment. "How much older is Chris than you?"

"Four years. Why?"

Kayla hesitated. "My new boyfriend is eighteen. He has a driver's license."

Was she looking for approval? "How do your parents feel about you dating a boy three years older than you?"

"Dad would freak if he knew, and I haven't told Mom. Although, she probably wouldn't care."

Time to take on the role of big sister. "Do you mind if I give you a little advice?"

"If you're gonna tell me how older boys sometimes take advantage of younger girls, I already know."

Hopefully not from personal experience.

"Maybe he'll drive me to Blue Ridge sometime soon."

Was a driver's license the reason for the new relationship? "Or better yet, how about Chris, Ryan, and I come and visit you in Nashville early next year?"

Kayla's eyes widened. "Really?"

Wendy faced her husband, her brows raised.

He signaled a thumbs-up.

"Definitely."

"Cool. Anyway, I hope you have a fun day."

"You too, sis." Wendy ended the call and set her phone on the end table. "Did Kayla seem a little sad?"

"She's fifteen. Who can tell?"

"Good point."

Eager to celebrate Thanksgiving before Abby left to spend the afternoon and evening with Tommy's family, Erica set four plates of chocolate-chip pancakes with a side of crisp bacon on the table.

After drizzling syrup over her pancakes, Abby cut a piece and popped it in her mouth. "Scrumlicious."

Amanda bit a chunk of bacon. "I talked to Morgan a few minutes ago. She and Kevin arrived in New Orleans late last night."

Abby swirled a chunk of pancake in a puddle of syrup. "Do you mind if I ask you both a serious question?"

Amanda shrugged. "As long as it's not about dating, I'm game."

Erica eyed her daughter. "What's on your mind?"

"For the six years Gunter was illegally married to both of you and the three he was also illegally married to Wendy, did you find it strange how many times he missed Thanksgiving and Christmas? That he never spent both at home the same year? I understand why Wendy might have been gullible, but you two are smart women."

"Talk about a tough question." Amanda laid her fork down. "At some point during our fourth year together, I concluded that I had made a huge mistake, especially since Morgan never warmed up to him. Truth be told, the man I'd known as Paul Sullivan provided us a comfortable lifestyle, so I accepted his excuses and didn't mind him being away during holidays."

Erica wrapped her fingers around her coffee cup. How much could she reveal without coming across as foolish or laying a guilt trip on her child? "During the last couple of years we were together, I suspected he was having an affair."

Abby stared at her, her eyes brimmed with tears. "You love me so much you stayed in an unhappy marriage to protect the lifestyle Gunter gave us, didn't you?"

"I wanted to give you so much more than I could on my own, sweetheart."

"You've given me something far more precious than anything money could ever buy." Abby reached across the table and touched Erica's arm. "Unconditional love and the freedom to follow my own dreams."

Erica's eyes teared up. "The day you were born was the most blessed day of my life."

Amanda sniffled. "What a special way to begin a day of thanks—in addition to savoring Abby's favorite breakfast."

An hour after gathering in the Armstrongs' dining room, Wendy patted her tummy. "This is the most fun Thanksgiving I've ever experienced. The meal was delicious, and the company is joyful."

"Perfect timing, Wendy." Keith leaned forward. "Every Thanksgiving before enjoying dessert, we go around the table and share what we have been most grateful for during the past year. Today, our daughter will begin our family tradition." He clicked his glass to Allison's.

A smile spread over the new mother's face. "Every time I deliver a precious baby into this world, I find joy in playing a small role in the beginning of a tiny human's first moment outside the womb." Allison faced her husband. "Not until another doctor placed my newborn child on my chest did I fully understand the true miracle of God's most precious gift. I love you and our daughter more than words can express." She clicked her glass to Mark's.

His eyes remained focused on Allison. "I didn't think I could love my wife any more than I did the day before our baby was born. From the moment I held Ellie in my arms, not only did I fall in love with my new daughter, but my love for the woman I married grew by leaps and bounds." He kissed Allison's cheek, then turned and clicked his glass to Amanda's.

"There have been so many blessings, including moving to Blue Ridge and creating a business with the best partners in the world. Above all, I'm thankful my daughter married her soulmate." She clicked her glass to Linda's.

"First, I'm grateful our son fell in love with a beautiful young woman who has made his life complete and brought Amanda and Erica into our lives. Second, our family is blessed with the birth of two precious grandchildren who will grow up in homes overflowing with love." Linda tapped her mother-in-law's glass.

"As matriarch of this family, I'm grateful God has given me another year to enjoy my children, my grandchildren, my great-grandchildren, and the new members of the Armstrong clan. I'm also thankful I can still paint my own toenails."

"Something I couldn't do during the last four months of my pregnancy," added Allison.

Susan tapped Erica's glass.

"Last year when my daughter and I ate Thanksgiving alone in our Asheville house, little did we know how much our lives were about to change. Today, I am eternally grateful God spared her life. Our heavenly father has something amazing planned for her future, just as he has for each of us." Erica lifted her glass to Chris.

"The day I met Wendy in Blue Ridge Inn's dining room, I was attracted to her beauty and zest for life. It didn't take long to realize there was so much more to this amazing woman." Chris's eyes met Wendy's. "Falling in love with you and adopting Ryan as my son have blessed my life more than I ever imagined possible." He tapped his glass to hers.

Overwhelmed with emotion, Wendy swallowed the lump in her throat. "All I ever wanted when I was growing up was a family who loved me and cared for each other. Now I'm married to a man I love with every fiber of my being, and who's an awesome daddy to our little guy. As an added bonus, he comes with a loving family who has welcomed me and my best friends with open arms. It's as if after waiting all these years, I finally ended up with the grand prize."

Chris stroked her cheek "Your wit and unique perspective are two more reasons I'm wild about you."

Allison cleared her throat. "Maybe you two should get a room."

Chris's eyes remained focused on Wendy. "Do you suppose my sister is a bit jealous?"

"She gave birth less than a week ago, so I suspect she's eager for more than a little kissing."

The entire family burst out laughing.

Wendy smiled at Chris. "Is this a good time to click my father-in-law's glass?"

He winked. "Definitely."

Wendy broke eye contact with her husband then turned toward Keith and tapped his glass.

"Welcoming Wendy, Erica, and Amanda into our family and becoming a grandpa to Ryan and Ellie top this year's list of blessings. Now I want to talk about next year." The senior Armstrong law partner set down his glass then folded his arms on the table. "The day our DA charged Jimmy Barkley with reckless endangerment, Linda and I began a serious conversation about what needed to be done beyond Chris delivering a not-guilty verdict."

"Please, Dad." Allison reached across the table corner and placed her hand on his arm. "Don't tell us you plan to run against Richard Watson."

"That man needs a challenger who can beat him."

Allison withdrew her hand. "Have you forgotten you had a heart attack?"

"Five years ago without a single episode since."

Allison jerked her head toward the other end of the table. "Are you going to let him do this, Mom?"

"We both appreciate your concern, honey, which is why we consulted with your father's cardiologist before we made a final decision."

Allison pointed her finger toward her brother. "You're his partner. Are you going to talk some sense into him?"

Chris faced his father. "What did your doctor tell you?"

"My ticker is good to go."

"Well then, I'd say Watson's days are numbered."

Allison slumped back in her chair.

Susan lifted her wine glass. "I propose a toast to our next district attorney."

Allison released a sigh before joining the rest of the family and raising her glass.

Following dinner while the family gathered in the den, Wendy pulled Chris aside. "You're conflicted over your dad's decision, aren't you?"

He hesitated, as if struggling to find the right words. "Chances are he'll beat Watson, which means at some point I'll be forced to oppose Dad in a courtroom."

Wendy looped her arm around Chris's elbow. "At least we have a year before the election."

"There is that."

Chapter 31

A family of deer grazed in the front yard as unseasonally warm weather and a cloudless sky ushered in the last month of the year.

"What a contrast from last December."

Amanda spun toward Erica. "Between now and Christmas, there's a zero chance a single snowflake—much less a blizzard—will accost North Georgia."

"One more reason our Blue Ridge Inn weekend will be far more enjoyable than last year."

"Speaking of inn weekends, I came across something interesting a few minutes ago." Amanda returned to the desk and tapped her laptop keyboard. "Check out this February reservation."

Erica leaned close to the laptop. "Donna Hewitt for a party of two?"

"Look at the address."

"Hilton Head. Are you thinking this woman is related to Douglas Hewitt?" Erica's brows shot up. "What if she's his wife?"

"Wendy never told us her father's address, and the reservation doesn't name the other person, so we have no way of finding out one way or the other."

Erica straightened. "Should we tell Wendy?"

Amanda shook her head. "If this woman is her father's wife, all sorts of questions will surface, including whether or not he knows about the reservation."

"On the other hand, if Donna has nothing to do with Douglas Hewitt, Wendy will face one more disappointment. I suggest we hold back from telling her until the week before this mystery guest shows up. Although—" Erica tapped her chin. "Wendy might stumble across the name on her own."

"Between taking care of a new baby, adjusting to married life, and continuing her online courses, I doubt she'll take time to do much more than review the number of reservations."

"You're right." Erica glanced at her watch. "Have you read Faith's text telling us we can check in at one?"

"A couple of minutes ago."

Millie meandered in from Hilltop. "When are you two leaving?"

"As soon as we finish packing." Amanda closed her laptop. "Erica and I appreciate you covering for us, Millie."

"Bernie's staying late for the next two days, so you can relax and enjoy the weekend."

"We will." Amanda waved over her shoulder as she headed toward her room.

Forty-five minutes later the three wives club members gathered on Blue Ridge Inn's back porch. Wendy stooped to pet the resident cat while Amanda rang the bell.

Faith pulled the door open. "Three of our all-time favorite guests. We still miss the miniature snowman in our freezer."

Amanda chuckled. "No chance we'll create a new snow creature during this stay."

"Or end up stranded." Faith grabbed a key then stepped outside and opened the door to the Lodge Suite. "Welcome to our newest addition."

Amanda stepped into the space that had served as Mountain Mama's Coffee Lounge before the owner moved to a new location. Two king-size beds with navy blue spreads hugged the back wall. A beige suede sofa and chair created a cozy seating area in front of the fireplace.

Wendy walked in and set a box on the island where customers had previously placed orders. "Truffles from my handsome husband instead of a con man."

Erica set a bottle of Champagne and a bottle of chardonnay beside the truffles. "Two more contributions to our first annual celebration of life after Gunter."

Amanda opened the back door and breathed in the fresh fall air. "The weather's warm enough to enjoy the screened porch for a while."

"The perfect place to unwind." Wendy set her suitcase on a luggage stand. "We can unpack later. For now, why don't we enjoy a glass of bubbly."

Amanda hoisted her bag onto one of the beds. "Given it's cocktail hour somewhere, we might as well begin celebrating."

"I'm game." Erica moved the wine to the mini fridge then uncorked the Champagne and filled three wine glasses.

Amanda carried her glass out to the porch and settled on a cushioned chair while Erica followed and sat on the chair beside her. "I have a proposal."

"Something official or fun?" Wendy dropped onto a matching love seat across from her partners.

"A little of both. Why don't we replace 'Exclusive Wives' Club' with a title that reflects who the three of us are now, versus who we were a year ago."

Erica nodded. "Especially since Wendy is now an honest-to-goodness wife."

Amanda took a sip of Champagne. "Maybe we'll have one more before the end of next year."

Wendy's brows raised. "Did Brad propose?"

Erica held up her splayed left hand. "Do you see a ring on my finger?"

"No."

"Well, there you go." Wendy curled her foot under her knee. "Our little club consists of one wife, one girlfriend, and one...hmm. How should we classify you, Amanda?"

"As a contented, single forty-four-year-old president and innkeeper."

"Maybe Erica and I should make it our mission to find the perfect man to keep you warm during cold winter nights."

Amanda laughed. "Have you been talking to Miss Gertie?"

"Who?"

"Kevin's grandmother. She made the same ridiculous comment. Trust me, my down comforter keeps me plenty warm."

Wendy swallowed a sip of Champagne. "Back to your suggestion. Instead of racking our brains for a name, why don't we wait and see what surfaces after we share stories for two days."

Amanda set her glass on the coffee table. "Let's start this party by sharing a happy memory from our childhoods."

"Great idea." Erica tipped her glass toward Awesam's president. "Starting with you."

"All right." Amanda crossed one leg over the other. "After my father abandoned my mother and me, we barely scraped by."

Wendy's eyes widened. "That's a happy memory?"

"Chill. I'm getting to the good part. On my eighth birthday, Mom and I rode the bus downtown. After indulging on ice cream sundaes, we boarded the St. Charles streetcar—"

Wendy's head tilted. "The same streetcar that rode by your last house in New Orleans?"

"Yes. Anyway, we rode for hours pretending we were flying on a magic carpet. We made up stories about visiting faraway places—some I had never heard of. Despite working two jobs to keep food on our table, my mother managed to create magical moments with nothing more than a few dollars and her imagination." Amanda thumped Erica's arm. "Your turn."

"My family also barely scraped by. Although the only imagination my mother had was how to avoid staying sober."

Wendy scoffed. "Do all your memories also begin with a negative?"

"I'm just saying...never mind." Erica paused. "All of my clothes were from Goodwill's double markdown racks." She eyed Wendy. "I'm giving you back story."

"Got it."

"During one of those Goodwill shopping trips, I found a dollar bill on the floor. No one else was around, so Mother told me I could buy any item I could find for a buck. As a seven-year-old kid who had never had a nickel to my name, I searched the toy aisles from top to bottom. All of a sudden, there it was—a sparkly princess crown, like a tiara. I grabbed it off the shelf, carried it straight to the checkout counter, and laid down my money. The cashier checked the tag then told me I needed twenty-five more cents. I must have looked up at her with the saddest eyes she'd ever seen because she leaned down and said, 'Today's your lucky day. We just marked this treasure down to a dollar.'" Erica smiled. "Every time I wore that crown, I pretended I was the richest little girl in the world."

Wendy pressed her hand to her chest. "I believe one of the reasons we have become a family is because we each struggled through difficult childhoods."

Erica nodded toward Wendy. "Your turn to tug on our heartstrings."

"You know *Sugar Snow* is the only treasure I have from my childhood. In my second foster home, I shared a room with a boy who was eight, a year older than me. He didn't know how to read, so every night I read my book out loud and began teaching him some of the words—me a seven-year-old teaching a kid how to read. Anyway, one day he read the story all the way through. When he closed the book, he thanked me for making him smart, and he kissed me. My first kiss wasn't romantic, but memorable."

Amanda pressed her hand to her chest. "Preston was my first passionate kiss."

Wendy snickered. "We already know Preston was the love of your life. Now tell us about the *first* boy who kissed you."

Amanda dug deep into her memory bank. "I had a third-grade crush on a kid named Davey. One day during recess, he climbed up the slide behind me. At the top, I glanced over my shoulder and asked him to be my boyfriend. He kissed me, then pushed me so hard I flew off the end of the slide and skinned both knees. Thus ended the shortest romance in history."

Erica laughed. "My first romance lasted a bit longer. Rusty's family lived on the bottom floor of our apartment building. His hair was as red as yours, Amanda. We were in the same second-grade class. One day when we were sitting on our building's front steps he kissed my cheek and told me I was the prettiest girl in Baltimore. I was smitten. Until a few weeks later when a family moved into the apartment across from his. Needless to say, I was replaced by a twelve-year-old blonde bombshell." Erica smiled at Wendy.

"Instead of replacing us, Gunter added a gorgeous blonde to his exclusive wives club."

Amanda chuckled. "Now that we've transitioned to the reason we all met, what's your most memorable moment of our first weekend here, Erica?"

"Hands down, indulging on Wendy's truffles in the inn's library that first night and sharing intimate details about our lives. I imagined we were sisters in an exclusive college sorority. Little did I know how exclusive."

"No kidding." Amanda turned toward Wendy. "My favorite memory was watching your eyes light up every time you created a miniature snow creature."

"You and Erica were good sports to go along with my crazy idea." Wendy's chin dropped to her chest. "After all those years I spent in foster homes, I came to expect ridicule as a way of life. Then that first day when the three of us shopped and my credit card was rejected—" She lifted her chin. "You have no idea how deeply you touched my heart when you pretended you hadn't heard."

Amanda lifted her glass. "A toast to us—three unlikely strangers who have redefined family."

During the rest of the day and through the evening, the Awesam partners laughed and cried while sharing poignant memories from their pasts and exciting visions of their future. Sunday, they strolled through downtown and lunched at Southern Charm. By checkout time Monday morning, they had settled on the name 'Victory Sorority' to replace 'Exclusive Wives' Club.'

Chapter 32

Wendy's heart overflowed with love as she smiled at Ryan peering up at her from his changing table. "Last December I dreamed of a baby girl wearing a frilly dress to celebrate her first Christmas." She slid her little guy's arms into his new outfit. "Now I'm the luckiest mommy in the whole world dressing my precious baby boy in his first tuxedo."

Chris slid his arm around Wendy's shoulders. "And I'm the luckiest daddy in the world to share Christmas with my beautiful wife and handsome son."

Wendy lifted Ryan into her arms. "Should we give your daddy his present now?"

Their little guy babbled.

"Right answer." After she carried their son into the great room and placed him in his baby swing, Wendy sat on the floor between the Christmas tree and the fireplace. Their black Lab sprawled on his belly beside the presents.

Chris sauntered over, dropped beside Wendy, and stroked Duke's muzzle. "Sorry, boy, this year the first present goes to the newest member of our family." He removed a ring of colorful loops from a gift bag and held it in front of his son. Ryan wrapped his fingers around a loop and drew the toy straight to his mouth. Chris chuckled. "Our boy's stamp of approval." He removed a wrapped gift and placed it in front of their four-legged family member. "Now it's your turn."

Duke tore the paper off the giant chew bone, then carried his gift to his favorite spot in front of the French doors.

"I wonder if Abby wrapped a present for Dusty?" Wendy pulled out a large box and placed it in front of Chris. "I hope you like what I picked out."

"I'll love anything you give me, angel." He ripped off the paper then lifted the lid off the box and pulled out a black leather jacket. "Wow. Talk about luxurious."

"It's lambskin, and I bought it with money I earned as Awesam's CFO."

"The best gift ever." Chris leaned close and kissed Wendy's cheek. "Are you ready to open your gift?"

"More than ready."

"All right then." He placed a shoebox-sized package on Wendy's lap.

She peeled off the paper and opened the box revealing another wrapped box. "My first Christmas surprise—a present in a present." Wendy giggled as she unwrapped the second box and discovered a third wrapped gift. "Let me guess. There's a note in this box telling me the real gift is still under the tree."

Chris winked. "Maybe."

She peeled off the paper and stared at a turquoise Tiffany box. Her eyes met Chris's.

"Go ahead and open it."

Wendy lifted the lid. A ring featuring a pale blue stone partially encircled with a curved row of leaf-shaped diamonds nestled on black velvet.

"The stone is an aquamarine to match your beautiful blue eyes."

She held up her right hand.

Chris slipped her gift onto her finger. "A perfect fit."

Tears of joy pooled as Wendy splayed her fingers. "You're spoiling me."

He dabbed her cheeks. "You deserve to be spoiled." Kayla's ringtone sent Chris scrambling to the kitchen. He pressed the speaker and handed the phone to Wendy. "Merry Christmas, sis."

Kayla sniffled.

Wendy's brows furrowed. "What's wrong, honey?"

"This is my gift from Mom." Kayla held up her right hand displaying a ruby ring encircled with diamonds.

"Oh my gosh, what a beautiful gift."

"You don't understand. Other than her wedding ring, this is Mom's favorite piece of jewelry. Why would she give it to me now?"

At a loss for words, Wendy exchanged a glance with Chris.

He moved close to the phone. "I'm not an expert on mothers, but as an attorney who sometimes deals in family law, I'd say she gave you her ring because she loves you with all her heart."

"Maybe you're right." Kayla swiped her fingers across her cheeks. "What did you give Wendy?"

"A ring because I love her."

The morning after celebrating Christmas Eve at Harvest on Main with her family, Amanda settled beside Monica Hartman on the green velvet sofa in Hilltop Inn's den. The crackling fireplace blaze added warmth to the cozy setting. "You and Adam were sweet to treat us to dinner last night."

"We've looked forward to spending Christmas with your family since Kevin and Morgan's wedding. Especially after you and I shared intimate details about our pasts during breakfast at Brennan's. I've been dying to tell you the latest news." A smile lit Monica's face. "Because of your inspiration, after devoting years to being a wife, a mother, and a New Orleans socialite, I've become a career woman."

"Wow. Congratulations."

"Thanks to my connections, a multi-national company hired me as their community liaison."

Adam ambled in from the foyer. "The position is critical to management's relationship with New Orleans." He sat beside his wife." I couldn't be prouder of this brilliant woman."

Monica patted his knee. "My sweet husband has supported me every step of the way."

"I always knew one day you would take advantage of your business degree."

The French doors swung open admitting a blast of cool air. Miss Gertie stepped in and peeled out of her coat then moved close to the fireplace. "Millie told me fascinating stories about her friendship with Eleanor Harrington, and how she became Hilltop's chef. Oh my goodness, her English country garden is as impressive as any I've seen back in New Orleans."

Millie's face beamed as she sidled beside her new friend and nodded toward the Christmas tree she'd decorated. "Gertie also appreciates traditional decorations and my angel topper."

Amanda chuckled. "Our talented chef and master gardener considers Hilltop's living room tree a bit too highfalutin for her taste. Even though guests at our holiday open house last weekend complimented both trees."

"Actually—" Millie switched on the multi-colored Christmas tree lights. "The blue and gold decorations and white lights have grown on me."

Morgan and Kevin meandered in from the foyer. "The breakfast buffet you set up in the dining room was delicious, Millie."

"Especially the cinnamon buns." Kevin licked his lips. "Best I've ever tasted."

"Wait until you taste my award-winning chocolate peppermint cake. I baked two and took one to my son and daughter-in-law's last night."

Morgan patted her belly. "I suspect Kevin and I will gain at least five pounds before we drive back to Atlanta."

Multiple footsteps struck the foyer floor. "Merry Christmas, everyone."

Amanda stood and spun toward the new arrivals. "Monica, Adam, and Gertie, meet the Armstrong family." Following introductions, Amanda and Linda held their grandbabies while Wendy showed off her Christmas present.

Millie gripped Wendy's right hand. "How many carats is that fancy blue stone?"

"It's a two-carat aquamarine."

"All I have to say is lawyers must make a lot of money."

Susan chuckled. "Coming from a family of reputable attorneys, I guarantee they earn every dollar."

Millie ambled over and linked arms with Miss Gertie and Susan. "Why don't the three of us senior citizens enjoy some eggnog spiked with rum and brandy while we become better acquainted?"

Kevin's grandmother patted Millie's hand. "I like the way you think."

After Erica unlocked Hilltop's French door, Brad pushed both halves open. Tommy maneuvered Abby's wheelchair over the threshold and into the den. Morgan introduced the newcomers to Kevin's parents.

Adam clasped his hand on Brad's shoulder. "I hear you were a champion football coach."

"A few years back. Chris was one of my star players, and Tommy helped lead our basketball team to victory before he graduated."

"Three accomplished athletes." Adam withdrew his hand. "I'm eager to hear your opinions about this year's college playoffs."

While the men launched a discussion about sports and headed to the living room, the women—minus the three seniors—gathered around the fireplace. After Abby lifted her body onto the sofa beside Erica, Morgan moved the wheelchair aside then settled beside Amanda.

Monica scooted to the edge of her chair. "Morgan told us you're a child psychology major, Abby."

"Yes, ma'am."

"Congratulations for choosing such an important career path."

Monica's comment began a lively conversation about careers, family, and the joy of grandchildren until Millie escorted Susan and Gertie back to the den. Hilltop Inn's chef stood in front of the fireplace. "Okay, ladies, I have a question I doubt any of you can answer."

Amanda laughed. "How much spiked eggnog have you consumed?"

"Just two little cups. Here's the question." Millie slid one hand into her pants pocket. "What do a retired obstetric nurse, a New Orleans socialite, and a chief information officer have in common?"

Linda snapped her fingers. "They all have wonderful families?"

"True, but that's not the answer. Any more guesses?"

Wendy crossed one leg over the other. "We give. What do those three ladies have in common?"

"First, all three love to cook. Second—" An impish grin lit Millie's face as she pulled her pistol out of her pocket. "They all carry the same brand of firearm."

Monica burst out laughing. "My mother-in-law has finally met her match."

While the pistol-packing mamas joined the conversation, Amanda placed Ryan in Abby's arms then motioned to Erica and Wendy. They followed her into the dining room.

Erica eyed Awesam's president. "This is a strange time to convene a board meeting."

"Not when I'm curious about Millie's spiked eggnog." Amanda filled three glass cups. "Besides, I've been dying to ask about that gorgeous necklace you're wearing."

Erica fingered the diamond heart below her throat. "Brad's Christmas gift."

"Even though he didn't give you an engagement ring, a heart necklace is a clear indication of what's coming in your future."

Erica rolled her eyes. "Don't go jumping to conclusions."

"I'm just saying Brad has the same adoring expression when he looks at you as Chris has when he gazes at Wendy."

"Whatever happens between now and next Christmas, I'm glad I'm a member of our exclusive victory sorority." Wendy clicked her cup to Erica's then to Amanda's. "Here's to a new year filled with new adventures and mind-blowing miracles."

Thank you for reading Blue Ridge series book four. Books five, six, and seven will publish in 2025. If you're not already one of my newsletter friends, sign up now and you'll receive updates on the release dates. I'll also send you a link for a free eBook copy of my standalone novel Jenny's Grace. https://www.sub scribepage.com/pat-nichols-newsletter

If you'd like to read a completed series check out The Secret of Willow Inn, book one in the Willow Falls series. In 2024 the series was republished by Armchair Press. The original publication of book one had 795 Amazon reviews. https://www.amazon.com/Secret-Willow-Inn-Falls-Book-ebook/dp/B 0D8WRJDN1/ref

Afterword

Little did I know ten years ago when I finished writing my first manuscript what the future held. Now with my twelfth published novel, I'm blessed to have wonderful friends sharing this amazing journey with me.

My beta readers, Pat Davis, Carlene Dunn, Beverly Feldkamp, Kitty Metzger, Kathy Warner, and CJ Bruce provide valuable feedback and suggestions before the final editing process.

My editor and mentor, Sherri Stewart, who's also a multi-published author, always makes my books better.

Ane Mulligan and Creston Mapes are two award-winning authors who I frequently call on for advice and counsel.

John Lavin, owner of the real Blue Ridge Inn, and Jennifer Sullivan, owner of Owl's Nest are new friends who have graciously supported my quest to include real locations in this fictional series.

My launch team, some who have been with me from the beginning, help introduce each new book by posting reviews. I'm also grateful for every reader who takes the time to write a review or simply post a star rating. There is no better way to thank an author.

My friends at Word Weaver's International Greater Atlanta Area provide feedback and encouragement. A special thanks to Dana Turpin who opens her home to this wonderful group of authors.

From the beginning, my husband, Tim, and my beautiful family have encouraged me to follow my dreams.

Above all, I thank God for His unconditional love and grace and the gift of eternal life through Jesus.

Milton Keynes UK
Ingram Content Group UK Ltd.
UKHW032232011124
450424UK00008B/912